T0329292

"Lord Brockton," he said, eyes flashing in delight. "I'd heard you were in attendance this morning."

Matt said nothing. He trembled, barely able to hold back the almost uncontrollable rage that seethed through him.

"Come to watch the festivities, did you?" Creighdor taunted. "I didn't know you indulged in this kind of entertainment. People dying after pleading uselessly for their lives. That sort of thing." His grin broadened.

Matt looked away from his mortal enemy. "I have the map, Creighdor. Whatever secrets Scarlet Moon possessed will be mine soon enough."

"Will they now? After being hidden for thousands of years?"

"You appear not to have given up hope of finding that ship."

HUNTER'S LEAGUE

A Conspiracy Revealed

The Mystery Unravels

The Secret Explodes

His Legacy Avenged

HIS LEGACY AVENGED

MEL ODOM

SIMON PULSE
New York London Toronto Sydney

For my hard-working editor, Michelle Nagler. And to the Wednesday night writing class that keeps me on my toes: Jodi, Kathleen, Lulu, Kelly, and Dave, as well as Fran, who keeps things running smoothly.

SIMON PULSE
An imprint of Simon & Schuster Children's Publishing Division
1230 Avenue of the Americas, New York, NY 10020
Copyright © 2006 by Mel Odom
All rights reserved, including the right of reproduction in whole or in part in any form.
SIMON PULSE and colophon are registered
trademarks of Simon & Schuster, Inc.
Designed by Sammy Yuen Jr.
The text of this book was set in Palatino.
Manufactured in the United States of America
First Simon Pulse edition March 2006
10 9 8 7 6 5 4 3 2 1

Library of Congress Control Number 2005938222
ISBN: 978-1-4814-0157-9

Chapter 1

London, England
1887

Pale, ghost-white fog oozed down the throat of Old Bailey Street and skirled down the twisted alleys around Newgate Prison. Fine mist rode the fog and occasional moonlight burned the moisture silver. The streetlamps warred at regular intervals with the dark night.

Matt Hunter sat in the rear of a hansom cab and stared at an imposing stone structure. He couldn't shake the feeling of dread that raked jagged claws along his spine. Newgate Prison was a miserable hunk of mortar and stone, a long, rectangular box rooted at the side of the street. Its presence within the city served to intimidate and remind those who operated outside the law that justice would be swiftly dispensed in a harsh manner.

Guilty men and women were no longer publicly hanged there, Matt knew. That cruel practice, performed on Mondays and always before a huge crowd that brought picnic baskets and children for the entertainment, had stopped in 1868. However, the condemned were still hanged *inside* the dismal edifice at regular intervals.

"Lord Brockton."

At the mention of his hereditary title, Matt glanced over at his companions. Until the last few months, Lord Brockton had always been his father's title.

"Yes," Matt answered quietly.

"Are you quite all right?" Medgar Thaylor sat across from Matt. Dressed impeccably, Thaylor was a large, capable man in his early seventies. He possessed a thick mane of hair, jutting side-whiskers, and an impressive mustache, all the color of ash. His keen gray eyes missed nothing.

"I am." Matt hoped the lie would hold. He didn't feel all right, but he didn't want to show any sign of weakness. Thaylor might feel emboldened enough to once more suggest—strenuously—that the mission they were on be put to rest and forgotten.

Thaylor leaned across the seat and glared at the prison. "This is an unforgiving place. The men and women, through whatever tragic circumstance brings them here, are dealt with even more harshly inside these walls. Few emerge unscathed. Doubtless, you will not emerge unscathed either, I'm afraid." He paused. "Have you ever had cause to visit this place?"

Matt stared at the stone walls slick with mist. "No."

"Forgive my bluntness, my lord, but 'twould be better were you to forget the unhappy happenstance that brings you here now."

"I appreciate both your concern and your candor, Mr. Thaylor."

"But you will not give up your quest? Nor tell me exactly what it is that you are here for?"

"No, sir. Not yet." Matt felt guilty over the last part. Medgar Thaylor had been the barrister for Roger Hunter, the previous Lord Brockton, his whole life. The two men had been good friends as well as doing business together.

Thaylor took in a deep breath through his nose, then blew it out.

The hansom cab rocked to a stop at the street corner. The horse stomped and blew, shaking its head. Unleashed on the empty street, the clinking harness sounded loud and unnatural.

Paul Chadwick-Standish opened the door before the driver could hurry to it. Like Matt, Paul wore a black suit and tails, making as much of their standing as young gentlemen as they could. Matt, though, could never pull off the elegance and disdain that Paul wore like armor.

A shock of curly red hair peeked from under Paul's top hat as he opened a black bumbershoot to ward off the falling mist. He was thin and graceful, excellent out on the dance floor, and dangerous with a fencing épée in hand.

Matt stepped out of the cab and clapped his hat on. He preferred to go bareheaded, but the top hat served to remind prison officials that he was a lord, a member of the aristocracy. He was broad shouldered and tall, with thick black hair and emerald-green eyes that he'd inherited from his mother.

The driver stood before them, a gaunt man a full head taller than Matt's six feet. He was in his forties. His scarred face spoke of hard years and great danger. His eyes roved constantly, watching the street and the shadows.

Matt knew that sudden death awaited his slightest misstep if Lucius Creighdor had caught wind of his plans this night. Creighdor had been Matt's father's enemy for years. Roger Hunter had pursued Creighdor throughout London, seeking revenge for the murder of Matt's mother.

Lady Brockton had been found horribly murdered and mutilated down near Canterbury. Officially, Angeline Hunter's death remained unsolved, but for a time, Roger Hunter had been a chief suspect. Everyone believed that Lady Brockton's murder had unhinged her husband.

Even Matt had believed his father mad. But that was before Matt had seen Creighdor receive a mysterious shipment from a ship called *Saucy Lass*. Shortly after that, Matt watched his father die at the hands of a vicious gargoyle controlled by Creighdor. The man had replaced some of the city's macabre decorations with ones that came to life under his control. Matt still didn't know the secret of the animated gargoyles, but he knew of the strange metal boxes and wiring concealed within.

"I'll keep a weather eye peeled out 'ere, right enough, guv." The driver touched his hat. "Won't nothin' be amiss when you should return. I give you me word on that."

"Thank you, Joseph. I can't say how long we'll be."

Joseph shrugged. "Ain't gonna matter none. When you get back, me an' ol' Bessie'll be waitin', we will." He touched his hat in a two-fingered salute.

"Just you make sure you don't get your throat slit in the dark," Matt said quietly so Thaylor wouldn't overhear.

"Oh, an' there ain't gonna be no worries there, they ain't." Joseph grinned and winked. "I been takin' care of meself for a long time, I 'ave."

Matt nodded, then took the lead toward the prison. He scanned the building's roofline. No gargoyles lounged there.

Grim-faced men in dark uniforms guarded the prison entrance.

Paul leaned in close to be heard. "Matt."

"Yes?"

"You do know what we're doing, right?"

Matt walled away the small insecurity he felt. He'd chosen his course of action. "Of course."

"Good." Paul didn't sound relieved. "I was just checking."

Matt stepped into the alcove.

"Visitin' hours is over," growled one of the guards. He clutched the police nightstick hanging from his belt. He was thick and beefy.

"I'm here by special appointment." Matt locked eyes with the man.

"Beggin' yer pardon, sir, but they ain't no such thing as a—," the guard began.

Medgar Thaylor imposed himself between Matt and the guard. "Do you know how to read?"

The guard grimaced. His pride overcame whatever feelings of caution he had. "Got better things to do with me time than learn to read. I'm a workin' man, I am."

"Would you recognize the Lord Mayor's signature when you saw it?" Thaylor demanded, shaking the paper he'd brought with him.

An uneasy look crossed the guard's moon face.

"If you can't," Thaylor went on, bringing all the force he could in his words, "then I suggest you contact a superior right away who can, if you want to save the employment you pride yourself on."

The guard worked his jaw for a moment, then nodded. "Yes, sir." He went to the door and shouted through a brass speaking tube.

A few minutes later, a younger man with the air of a clerk showed up. Thaylor impressed upon him the paper that he carried. The prison official stepped close to one of the lanterns beside the door and quickly read the note.

When he was finished, he glanced at Thaylor. "I'm Danner."

Thaylor quickly introduced himself, then Lord Brockton and Paul.

Consternation tightened Danner's face. "This is highly unusual."

"Quite," Thaylor agreed.

"Might I inquire as to the nature of this late call?" Danner asked.

"You already have, Mr. Danner," the barrister said. "Unfortunately, neither I nor my associates will answer anyone's questions. The signature on that piece of paper you're holding assures us of that."

If Danner felt any rebuke, he didn't show it. He nodded and ushered them into the building. "You realize, of course, I can't guarantee you or your associates safe passage."

"Understood." Thaylor took the lead. "We shall require a room in which to conduct the interview."

"Rooms are in scarce supply." Danner fell into step beside Thaylor.

"You seem an able fellow," Paul said pleasantly. "I'm rather certain you'll find something."

Danner summoned three guards in the hallway. Carrying truncheons, the men gathered round.

"An escort, Mr. Robbins, if you please," Danner said.

"Of course, sir."

Matt studied the roughhewn men. Judging from the scars on their faces and hands and the wary looks in their eyes, they were all used to violence. Matt knew that Danner hadn't summoned them to act as guards, but rather in their capacity as jailers.

They were promptly shown to a small, square office in the basement. The room had no windows, only a small desk and a chair. Scars and wear marred the aged stone floor.

"Will there be anything else?" Danner stood stiff-necked in the doorway. He clasped his hands behind his back.

"A pot of strong tea." Thaylor sat at the desk. "And three more chairs."

"Very well, sir." Danner nodded.

"I'd also like to see the prisoner straight away. Time is of the essence."

"Yes, sir."

Time is of the essence, Matt thought with a sour sickness at the pit of his stomach. In three days, the man they'd come to see was going to hang by the neck until dead.

Less than twenty minutes later, Cyrus Stewart entered the small room. Chains bound his wrists and ankles.

He was gaunt and unkempt, bowed from a

harsh life spent with misfortune. His ratty beard hung to the middle of his bony chest. He possessed a narrow, pinched face with squinty eyes. A scar outside his right eye pulled the lid even tighter.

"Mr. Stewart?" Thaylor didn't rise from his chair.

From beneath matted hair, Stewart's eyes roved the room. They stopped on Matt. "You would be Lord Brockton's son, then?"

"I would," Matt answered.

"You got me message?"

"I did." The telegram was folded neatly inside Matt's jacket.

Stewart stood in the doorway, somehow nearly filling it despite his emaciation. "I sent word nearly a week ago. Cost me a lot to send that telegram." Each word carried a full measure of guilt with it.

"See here, sir," Thaylor rebuked in a harsh voice. "Lord Brockton is here at his own sufferance. There will be no remonstration over timeliness or—"

"Please, Mr. Thaylor," Matt interrupted politely. "You've gotten me this far. Let me see if I can handle the rest."

Reluctantly, the barrister subsided.

"My apologies," Matt said. "Arranging this visitation has not been easy. Mr. Thaylor had to pull in several favors."

Stewart looked undecided. "I don't 'ave much

time. An' none of it to be wastin' sittin' an' wonderin' if you was even gonna come."

"I'm here now," Matt stated simply. He kept his impatience and curiosity in check. His war against Lucius Creighdor had taken a number of strange turns, this meeting just one more.

"An' come Monday," Stewart said, "you'd 'ave been too late."

"Mr. Stewart," Paul said softly.

The convict's eyes shifted to Paul. "An' who might you be?"

Paul doffed his hat with a flourish. "Paul Chadwick-Standish. At your service, sir."

"At me service?" A bitter smile quirked Stewart's thin lips.

Paul didn't flinch from the scathing tone. "As much as can be, yes."

"An' can ye spare me from the 'angman's gallows come Monday, Mr. Chadwick-Standish?"

"No." Paul's reply was flat and honest.

Stewart paled a little at the answer. His hands shook, causing the manacles to rattle. "Well, then," he croaked. He leaned against the doorway as if his legs were suddenly weak. "I wasn't one to 'old out any 'opes, I wasn't. Still . . ." His voice trailed off.

"You murdered a ship's captain," Matt said. "According to the records I've seen of you, you've been a sailing man all your life. You knew the penalty for mutiny."

"Aye." Stewart nodded solemnly and wiped

his eyes with a shaking hand. "That, I did, young Lord Brockton. But I 'ad no choice. Not really." He looked at Matt. "Did you read the particulars of me crime?"

"Only what the papers stated."

The prisoner cursed. "Them papers, they ain't but filled with twaddle, they ain't." His eyes took on a haunted look. "Come a blow down around the Cape of Good 'Ope. Bad a one as you'd ever want to face, it were. 'Ad us a new cap'n. A young'un. Still green all around an' 'im prideful as a peacock." His voice thickened and he had to clear it. "Like to lost the ship. Ever' man aboard 'er, we knew we 'ad to run with the storm. But Cap'n Dixon, 'e thought we should batten the 'atches an' ride it out."

Matt had never been caught out in the harsh weather he'd heard about while talking to the sailors who worked for his father. But they had told horrifying stories of storms that lashed the ocean seventy and eighty feet high.

"Well, we all knew that couldn't be done," Stewart went on. "But the cap'n, 'e got 'im a rifle an' offered to shoot any man what didn't follow 'is orders." He swallowed. "I was the only one standin' closest to the cap'n. I knew it all depended on me. I jumped 'im, knowin' I was facin' prison time an' a lashin' for sure. We fought for the rifle, an' not another man joined in. Only the cap'n, 'e 'ad 'im a belly gun, too. 'E was wild-eyed with fear. Weren't no reasonin' with 'im. I saw that. 'E pointed that pistol at me an' I 'ad no choice. I been in too many taverns, too many fights, not to fight for me life."

Matt felt sick to his stomach. The reports he'd read, and he'd heard in the taverns the sailors frequented had offered mixed views on what had happened. He wanted to believe Stewart's account.

"I 'ad me knife in me 'and afore I knew it," Stewart said in a whisper, "I opened up the cap'n's throat before I thought twicet about it. 'Eld 'im in me arms while 'e died an' the storm tried its best to smash us to pieces. Then I gave them orders that needed givin' an' I brought the ship through that gale."

Silence filled the small room for a time.

"But you brought the captain's body back with you," Thaylor said. "You could have heaved it overboard and claimed he'd been lost at sea."

"No, sir." Stewart shook his head. "That, I couldn't do. I sailed with Cap'n Dixon's father. Now in 'is prime, 'e was a sailin' man, 'e was. None finer. I couldn't just dump 'is boy over into the sea an' tell 'im a lie about 'ow 'e died. It were bad enough lookin' 'im in the eye an' tellin' 'im the truth."

"You could have jumped ship before you reached London," Paul pointed out.

Stewart nodded. "I could 'ave. Chose not to."

"Why?" Matt asked.

"'Ad to tell Cap'n Dixon what 'appened to 'is only son. Knew 'e wouldn't take the truth from no man on that crew but me." Pain filled Stewart's gaze as he looked at Matt. "An' I just up an' left like that—I wouldn't get to see me own family no more. I got a wife an' three little ones. I work 'ard to feed them, but I ain't no craftsman. Don't know nothin' but the sea. I was to just walk away from ever'thin' I know 'ere, I wouldn't get much work. I'd 'ave lost me family for sure. So I took me chances with the courts. Now they're gonna 'ang me for savin' that ship an' them men."

Two guards returned with a pot of tea and three chairs. They put the tea service on the desk, then spread the chairs around.

"I want Mr. Stewart's hands freed," Matt said.

The guards stared at him. "Sir," one of them said, "that's 'gainst regulations, it is."

"I'll assume responsibility." Matt didn't waver.

Hesitantly, one of the guards produced a key and removed the prisoner's manacles. "We'll be right outside," the guard said.

Matt closed the door to allow them more privacy.

Paul served the tea, giving a cup to Thaylor, then one to Stewart.

"Thankee," Stewart said. "Ain't had no tea since I been in 'ere."

"You've been in Newgate for over a month," Matt said.

"Aye, m'lord." Stewart held his teacup in both hands.

"Yet you only just now sent me a telegram." Matt took the paper from inside his jacket and unfolded it. He read the message once again.

LORD HUNTER STOP YOU DON'T KNOW ME, BUT I WAS A FRIEND OF YOUR FATHER'S STOP I SERVED WITH HIM IN THE CRIMEAN WAR STOP SOME MONTHS AGO YOUR FATHER SENT ME ON A MISSION THAT INVOLVED A MAN NAMED LUCIUS CREIGHDOR STOP I WAS THINKING YOU WOULD ALLOW ME TO TELL YOU WHAT I HAVE DISCOVERED STOP
I THINK I HAVE FOUND A SAILING VESSEL HE WAS SEARCHING FOR STOP PLEASE VISIT WITH ME AT YOUR EARLIEST CONVENIENCE STOP
YOUR SERVANT
CYRUS STEWART
NEWGATE PRISON

"Sendin' a message out of this place is powerful 'ard," Stewart said. "Especially puttin' it in the 'ands of the likes o' you. Them what arrested me didn't leave me any money. 'Ad to ask favors an' shift round a bit of contraband inside the prison to get the money I needed for the bribes an' such. I took a lot of risks." His eyes narrowed. "An' I 'spect you 'ave plenty of reason not to trust just any message you get."

"I do." Matt folded the telegram and put it away.

"I knowed your father," the prisoner said. "'E was a good 'un, 'e was. Didn't 'ear about 'is passin' till I was back in London. It was 'im I was first goin' to send that telegram to."

Matt locked down the pain he felt at his father's death. Months had passed, but it still hurt.

"I 'spect ye know who killed him," Stewart said. "'Twas the name Lucius Creighdor that brought ye here tonight, wasn't it?"

Matt locked eyes with the man. "I was with my father when he was murdered. Lucius Creighdor ordered the deed done."

Stewart nodded. "Then ye've got a fire in yer 'eart, don't you?"

"I will see my father avenged," Matt replied. "Or die in the attempt."

"I can see that in ye." Stewart raised a hand and scratched at his shaggy beard. "I would ask a boon of ye."

"If I can."

"After I'm gone, won't be nobody to look after me family. I've got a sister what's gone on to America with 'er 'usband. I would ask ye to provide passage for me wife an' children to America."

"I will see that it's done."

"An' one other thing." Stewart looked uncomfortable. "Maybe it won't be so easy to give."

Matt nodded. For the last week and a half he'd impatiently waited for Thaylor to get the interview granted.

"Come Monday," Stewart said, "they're gonna 'ang me by me neck till I'm dead." His voice broke a little, but he struggled to sound matter-of-fact. "They doesn't allow public 'angins no more, but there's some what can come in. If ye can see your way clear to it, I'd like ye to be there when they 'ang me."

Chapter 2

Cold dread slammed into Matt as Cyrus Stewart's request settled into his thoughts. He couldn't imagine what it would be like to witness a man being hanged.

Men, he immediately corrected himself. Newgate still hanged thirty to forty men a year. The possibility that Cyrus Stewart would hang alone was small.

But what choice do you have? Matt asked himself as he contemplated the horribleness of it all. *If Father and Creighdor felt driven to discover information about this ship, can you truly walk away without knowing?* He took a deep breath and slowly let it out.

"Are you prepared to withhold information from Lord Brockton should he not agree to honor your request?" Paul asked during the uncomfortable silence that followed.

Stewart's eyes remained locked on Matt's.

"Not at all, Mr. Chadwick-Standish. I will freely give 'im the information I 'ave no matter what 'e agrees to do. I just—" His voice broke. "I just don't want to die . . . alone. Without a friendly 'eart in the buildin'."

"You realize that given Lord Brockton's standing," Paul began, "he can hardly afford to appear—"

"I'll be there," Matt promised, and he felt as though he'd stepped into the unforgiving jaws of a bear trap.

"Matt," Paul protested.

"Lord Brockton," Thaylor said almost at the same time.

"It's done," Matt stated. "I've given my word to this man."

With a thankful smile, Stewart nodded. "I appreciate yer kindness, sir. Now let me tell ye about *Scarlet Moon*, the ship yer father was so interested in." He cleared his throat as if the discussion of his imminent death were a topic long past. "*Scarlet Moon* was a cargo ship, she was. 'Ad 'er a long an' illustrious string of voyages, she did. Mostly she was a cargo ship, an' mostly she carried legal freight all nice an' tidy as you please. But ever' now an' again, when time an' tide were against 'er, she flew the skull an' crossbones."

Matt spared a glance at Medgar Thaylor. The barrister listened intently. Thaylor hadn't known Matt was present during his father's murder, nor did he know of the war Matt and his friends had waged against Lucius Creighdor. Matt felt badly that the old man was getting pulled so deeply into the affair.

"Yer father, God rest 'is soul, took an interest in *Scarlet Moon*," the convict went on.

"My father barely mentioned that ship." Matt had found his father's notes on Lucius Creighdor soon after his father's murder. "He only wrote of it in passing, saying it was one of the leads he'd uncovered and wanted to follow up."

"Aye. 'E come to me to follow it up, 'e did."

"Why?"

"Because me gran'pap served aboard *Scarlet Moon*. 'E was a self-made man, 'e was an officer in the war 'gainst Napoleon. Got 'isself decorated at Waterloo. Afterward, 'e speculated some'at in shippin' an' the like. Was 'ow 'e came to know yer father."

"Why was my father interested in *Scarlet Moon*?"

"'E come to know of 'er because of me gran'-pap. By them days, gran'pap was a gentlemen of leisure, 'e was. Too old to go to sea, an' 'ad 'isself a big enough poke that 'e could sit back an' dicker tradin' an' such. That's 'ow 'e met yer father. Tradin'." A frown darkened Stewart's face. "Was the wreck of *Scarlet Moon* that broke 'im."

"When did the ship go down?"

"Over thirty years ago. In spring of fifty-five.

Come a squall out on the North Sea that sent 'er to Davy Jones' locker. Lost her bottom to a 'idden reef, she did. Only a few of the sailors what was on 'er survived. Ever'thin' else on 'er, me gran'-pap's goods an' that what yer father was interested in, was drunk down by them bitter cold waters. Gran'pap lost ever'thin' on that voyage. 'E was a gambler, 'e was. Couldn't back off of takin' a chance. Tried 'is 'and at piratin' again, but never was able to catch ahold of good luck."

Muffled conversation sounded out in the hall. Matt glanced at the door. Lucius Creighdor's grasp could reach into the prison as well. Matt felt naked without the .455-caliber Webley pistols he carried as a matter of course these days.

"Yer father," Stewart said, "'eard about that ship's cargo, 'e did."

"How?" Matt asked.

"Don't know." Stewart shrugged. "Me, I never asked. Yer father, 'e 'ad 'im a way of knowin' things, 'e did. Strange an' sometimes peculiar things. Never understood 'is interest, I didn't."

"What was in the cargo?" Paul asked.

"Don't know that neither. Not for certain. 'Eard from me gran'pap that it was some kind of ship. Somethin' what was made in Egypt."

"Egypt?" Matt repeated. "You're certain?"

"Aye. As certain I am as ye're standin' there, young Lord Brockton. 'Twas a ship. A model or some such. Though I don't know what kind it 'twas. An' it was made in Egypt. Part of some mummy's final restin' treasures or some such thing."

Matt's thoughts immediately flew to Pasebakhaenniut, the mummy Creighdor had been after those months ago when Lord Brockton had first brought his son into his mysterious investigations. In life, Pasebakhaenniut had been one of the Outsiders in ancient Egypt, godlike beings that returned from the dead and who helped teach the Egyptians about medicine and engineering, among other things.

As it turned out, Pasebakhaenniut's body held a number of secrets. Among them were the visions of old Egypt that shined from the mummy's eyes that Creighdor had triggered with a mysterious device. Oddest of all, though, was the mummy's unexpected and unexplained resurrection.

Only weeks ago, while attempting to decipher the secrets of the apparatus inside the mummy with generators, Pasebakhaenniut had somehow returned to life, breaking free and vanishing into the night. During the days that followed, the mummy hid in the shadows and struck with impunity, always at men who Matt discovered worked for Creighdor.

Lucius Creighdor—who seemingly was scared of nothing—feared the creature. Matt knew that. Pasebakhaenniut hunted Creighdor and warred with Creighdor's gargoyles. Several

of the animated stone creatures had been mysteriously shattered over the past few days.

"What happened to the Egyptian ship?" Matt
asked.

"Went down with *Scarlet Moon*, it did. Yer
father, 'e 'ad 'isself 'opes that it might turn up
someday." Stewart sipped his tea. "As it turns
out, mayhap it did."

"How?"

"A couple years ago, a dredger pulled up a
brass ship's bell what had *Scarlet Moon*'s name
struck on it," Stewart said.

Dredging took place all the time. Matt had
seen crew on his father's vessels that dredged.
Sailors, bored by long days of inactivity aboard
ship, simply dropped weighted nets to the bottom of the ocean in the hopes of bringing up
something worthwhile. Rarely did such things
occur, but they happened enough to keep sailors
open-minded about the attempts.

"The sailor kept the bell," Stewart went on,
"'opin' to ransom it back to the ship's company.
I 'eard about it an' went up to East Riding an'
found it in an 'ostelry where it was bein' used
as a decoration. Took me another eight months
to find a sailor what was with the swab that
dredged the bell up. By that time, word 'ad got
back to Lucius Creighdor that I'd found the
bell. 'Is men come lookin' for me, they did."

Matt shifted, anxious for the rest of the story.
"Why was Creighdor interested in the bell?"

"Not the bell—it were the wreck." Stewart rubbed his bloodshot eyes. "They wanted to know about the wreck. Where it were an' the like. I got the location of where them lads fished up that bell. Time I got back to London, though, yer father was dead. I didn't figure anyone else wanted to know about that wreck. Then, after I was locked up recently, I 'eard about ye. I thought maybe ye might want to know."

"I do," Matt said.

"Don't know the longitude an' latitude like a proper ship's officer or mate might know," Stewart said, "but I made a map. Got the area marked off an' the names of ship's crew that ye might be able to track down."

"Can I get it?"

"Aye. I made the map for yer father. Put it away in an 'idin' spot. Didn't know what else to do with it." Stewart cleared his throat. "There's some other things in with that map. I'd appreciate it if ye'd see my wife an' kids gets 'em."

"All I can give you is my word."

Stewart spat in his hand and offered it to Matt. Without hesitation, Matt took the hand and shook.

The convict grinned. "If'n yer word's as good as yer father's, it's good enough for me."

Pounding knuckles rattled the door. "Lord Brockton," Danner called irritably from the hallway. "You really should finish this visit. Even the names on that paper can grant you only so much leniency."

"Agreed, Mr. Danner," Matt called back. "I won't be but a moment more." He looked at Stewart. "I apologize."

Sour discomfort twisted the convict's pallid face. "Nothin' to forgive, young Lord Brockton. None of this business was yer doin'." He finished the last of his tea and set the cup aside. "Ye'll find the map an' them things at the Sailor's Rest down to East Smithfield." He added the address and continued in a whisper. "Ye'll find, in the basement, a loose floorboard in the southeast corner. I stocked there as a lad. Used to use it for all manner of things. Not all of them legal. If everythin's well, that map an' them things will still be there."

Matt shifted self-consciously. He wanted to go see if the map was still there. For at every turn, Creighdor remained ahead of him.

Getting to his feet, Stewart offered a small smile. "Sayin' good-bye under the circumstances is a bad thing, young Lord Brockton. Can't be anything but awkward."

"I know." Matt looked in the man's eyes and saw the haunted fear in them. "Is there anything I can do for you? Anything that you need?"

Newgate Prison not only locked up lawbreakers, it also made them pay for any privileges they got once inside. If a man didn't come in with money in his pocket, his family had to provide for him.

"Just ye take care of me family," the convict said. "As we agreed."

"I will." Matt shook the man's hand once more. Stewart's hand trembled slightly.

Thaylor called for the prison guards, who entered the room and quickly manacled Stewart again. They led him away.

Stewart shot a last look over his shoulder. "Till Monday, then, m'lord," he called. Desperation cracked his voice. "Bright an' early, if ye please."

"Till Monday," Matt echoed. He watched helplessly as the man vanished down the long, dark hallway.

Chapter 3

The Sailor's Rest was a three-story flop situated between a sailcloth shop and a cabinet warehouse. Built of weathered gray stone, the hostelry stood stiff as a pointing finger.

Matt sat inside the cab with Paul and Gabriel, another of his friends who had joined with him in the battle against his parents' murderer.

Thick dark hair trailed to Gabriel's shoulders. Heavy brows overhung his brooding black eyes. He was pale from his primarily nocturnal life, and wary from always having to look over his shoulder for policemen and recent victims. Short and wiry, Gabriel had the knack of disappearing into the shadows of the night in the space of a drawn breath. He wore dark clothing and fingerless woolen gloves.

During the years of their association, Matt had never discovered if Gabriel had a second name. Or even if Gabriel was his given name or surname. He'd grown up on the streets and taken to crime, becoming a pickpocket and a second-story man, as if he'd been born to it.

While Lord Brockton had been out chasing Lucius Creighdor and Matt had been left to his own devices, Matt had struck up a friendship with Gabriel. One that occurred after Gabriel had stolen from Matt, of course. Both of them had beaten the other nearly senseless in the fight that ensued. While talking afterward, they'd discovered a love of taking chances and living for moments of excitement.

Gabriel had Joseph drive past the building and pull the cab over to the side of the street. From the back of the coach they kept watch for a time. Nothing at the hostelry seemed amiss. All of the lanterns in the rooms were extinguished. Sailors returning late to their beds from the pubs and taverns might cause the only problem.

Finally, Gabriel climbed from the coach. "Joseph."

"Aye, sir," the coachman replied.

"You know my whistle."

"'Course I do."

Gabriel smiled. "If you 'ear it, come quick. Round to the back of the building. We 'ave trouble with the bobbies, I just want to get clear of the area. Anything else, do your best."

Reaching under his seat, Joseph produced a double-barreled fowling piece. "I'll keep a weather eye peeled, I will."

Gabriel led the way. Matt and Paul left their hats inside the coach, trusting their heavy outer coats to mask them in the darkness.

The cold had turned the mist to sleet, which peppered Matt's face. He pushed away all thoughts of discomfort and concentrated on the task at hand.

Through the back alley, piled high with garbage and infested with rats and the rancorous felines that preyed on them, Gabriel stopped at a slanted door that led down into the hostelry's basement.

"Delivery door," Gabriel announced. "Luck is with us."

Paul tapped his walking stick on the lock lying on the door. "Perhaps not so lucky."

Gabriel tested the lock attached to the heavy chain that sealed the door. "A trifle." He reached inside his coat. "Won't be but a shake of a lamb's tail." Lockpicks gleamed dully in his hand.

Matt kept watch over the alley. He had the creeping sensation that he was being watched. *One of Creighdor's goons?* he wondered. *Or Pasebakhaenniut?*

Both possibilities seemed equally disastrous.

Coaches passed out on the street. A few pedestrians hurried by as well, their collars turned up against the invading chill.

The lock clicked in Gabriel's hands, then lay open. "There you go, guv." Deftly, he threaded the chain from the door handle without making a sound, then deposited the length in his coat pocket. He looked up expectantly. "I don't suppose either of you thought to bring a light?"

"As breaking and entering and trespassing on the property of others has never been my forte or a dalliance," Paul said, "I find myself remarkably unequipped for such an endeavor."

Matt just shook his head. He hadn't thought things through that clearly.

Gabriel grinned. "Then you two best be glad you're tossin' the joint with the likes of me." He reached into another pocket and produced a small bull's-eye lantern. The lens was carefully covered to conceal and direct the illumination.

He lit the lantern with a lucifer, then closed the glass once more. A narrow beam shot out to interrupt the darkness cloaking the alley.

Matt helped pull the door open and they went down the short flight of steps into the basement. Gabriel's pocket lantern gave little relief.

"Take a minute," Gabriel advised. "Let your eyes adjust. Then we'll move."

Matt breathed slowly, willing himself to be calm. With the musty smell all around them and the shelves pressing in from the sides, he felt like he'd been buried deep within the earth. He quelled the panic that strove to break free within him.

Something darted across the floor in front of them.

Gabriel flicked the light after it, taking cover against one of the tall shelves that stood in rows throughout the room. Tiny eyes turned red under the lantern's glare.

"Don't get your knickers in a twist," Gabriel whispered. "It's only a rat."

The rat cowered behind an apple barrel. The creature was over a foot long from nose to tail, and was fat with its successes in the basement.

"Not the tidiest of places, is it?" Paul asked.

"But restful, no doubt," Gabriel said. "Not to mention cheap for them what would rather spend their 'ard-earned wages on a bottle of rotgut." He kept the lantern moving, sorting through the shelves' piles of refuse.

Over the years, the basement had become a repository for abandoned things as well as food. The shelves held boxes, jars, and bags of beans, potatoes, and other foods. Cheeses hung from the rafters, so low that Matt had to dodge them. But there were also clothes, bags, and duffels that had been left behind by men shanghaied for ships or arrested while in the city.

Gabriel moved forward, following the narrow tunnel of light. "What was the first thing I taught you about breakin' into a place, guv?"

"Always find the ways out," Matt answered. He pointed at the door to the upstairs room at the far end of the basement.

"Good," Gabriel congratulated him. "Glad to see all them lessons ain't been forgotten."

"He *taught* you to break and enter?" Paul sounded totally dumbfounded.

"Yes, I did. An' 'e's quite good at it, Matt is. Could 'ave been a proper thief if 'e'd put 'is 'ead to it."

"Whatever for?"

"Now an' again," Gabriel said, "afore this affair started up, 'is lordship would 'elp me re-acquire a thing or two that 'ad fallen into the wrong 'ands."

"You never told me about this," Paul lamented.

"It wasn't something that usually came up in conversation between us." Matt swept his gaze around. "The southeast corner?" He turned, orienting himself to the room. Then he pointed. "There?"

"Yes." Gabriel darted forward like a hound after prey.

Matt knew his friend had conjured up countless possibilities of what might be in Cyrus Stewart's hidden cache.

"Looks like it ain't been touched in ages." Gabriel removed a box of discarded and flea-infested clothing, then blew off a layer of dust.

"Cyrus Stewart has been away for a few months." Paul hunkered down beside the thief.

"'Old this, will you?" Gabriel handed Paul the lantern. "Keep the light on them boards."

Paul held the light steady as Gabriel ran his hands over the wooden flooring. The thief rapped his knuckles against the boards.

"Nice 'idin' place, it is. Dirty as things is

down 'ere, no one would look." Gabriel chose one of the boards, then fished a clasp knife from his pocket. He set the point at the space between the boards. "Cyrus Stewart didn't 'appen to mention any booby traps, now did 'e?"

"No." The thought hadn't even entered Matt's mind.

"Creighdor might 'ave gotten to 'im, mightn't 'e? Made 'im tell you what 'e told you?"

"To what purpose?" Paul asked.

"Why for the purpose of catchin' us in a sticky wicket, you nit," Gabriel growled, obviously ill at ease. "I got me an 'eadful of nasty ideas at the moment. Suppose 'e stuck one of them brain parasites in this 'ere 'idey-'ole? I might get it on me face, mightn't I? Then it would be all up in me brain in a trice."

The brain parasites were supposed to be creatures used by some of the Egyptians to control slaves. Creighdor had maintained a breeding factory for the unearthly monsters outside of London. He'd been quietly infecting the powerful and the wealthy that he could bring within reach of the physicians he controlled. Matt and his friends had found the factory and destroyed it, but that didn't mean the threat of the abominable creatures ended there.

"Carefully, then," Matt whispered. "If you want, I'll do it."

Without another word, Gabriel flipped the board over and exposed the dark hole.

Nothing leaped out at them.

Matt released the tense breath he'd been holding.

"Well, now," Gabriel sighed, "that's all for the good. Let me 'ave that lantern back, if you please." He took the lantern from Paul and shined it down into the hole. "Not much space 'ere."

"Enough for a map," Matt said.

"But little enough for any serious treasure." Disappointment stained Gabriel's words. He reached into the hole and withdrew a leather pouch. Passing it along to Matt, he held the lantern where they could all see.

Two ties held the pouch closed. Matt untied them, then lifted the flap. Inside was a tight roll of parchment, a few coins, folded pound notes, three gems, and two gold earrings.

"Not much in the way of a legacy for his wife and children, is it?" Paul asked.

"No." Matt removed the parchment and handed the pouch to Paul. "Look after this. When the time comes that we help Cyrus Stewart's family, make sure that the amount is more suitable. If they're going to make a proper start elsewhere, they'll need the means to do that."

"Agreed."

Unrolling the parchment, Matt gazed at it, making out the eastern England seacoast at once. Gabriel stepped behind him and better directed the lantern light.

The North Sea was clearly labeled. So was *Scarlet Moon*'s final resting place. The area wasn't marked by longitude or latitude, just as Cyrus Stewart had said it would not be. Rather, it was marked off by soundings and shore sightings, a lay seaman's designation rather than a trained mate or officer's.

"Do you really think you can find the ship-wreck from that?" Gabriel asked.

"I hope to."

"I've seen better directions scrawled on a privy wall, I 'ave."

Matt rolled the parchment again and tied it with a leather strap. He tucked it inside his jacket. "Let's get out of here."

Gabriel again took the lead and guided them back to the slanted door leading to the alley. Claws scratched the stone and shelving as rats scattered amid the rubble piles.

Just before Gabriel reached the door, someone opened it from outside. The light from a half-dozen lanterns blazed into the basement.

"Well, well," Lucius Creighdor purred. He stood out in the alley surrounded by a dozen stone-faced men. Angular and thin, Creighdor wore his black hair held back in a jeweled queue. "A few strands leaked down into his pallid face. His thin mustache and goatee were carefully groomed. The dark eyes belonged on a hunting falcon, cold, impersonal, and pitiless. He wore an elegant dark suit. Diamonds gleamed at his tie and cuffs. A strange-looking device dangled at the end of one arm. "This building is properly infested with vermin, isn't it?"

Creighdor's henchmen laughed in appreciation of his quick wit.

"So Cyrus Stewart told you his little secret, did he?" Creighdor asked.

Matt lifted one of the Webleys from his coat pocket and took aim at the center of Creighdor's chest, then squeezed the trigger.

In the confines of the basement, the detonation of the shell sounded like thunder. Creighdor staggered back two steps, hammered by the force of the round striking him. Incredibly, he glanced down to survey the damage. Green light flared on his chest, then his clothing turned dark again.

"How very, very stupid," Creighdor whispered. He jerked himself into motion, seemingly no worse for the wear. A small pistol slid free of his sleeve, and he drew the hammer back.

Before Creighdor could fire, Matt aimed at the man's head and fired. At almost the last moment, Creighdor jerked his head to one side. Matt's second shot caught Creighdor along the temple, splitting the skin and slamming into the brick wall on the other side of the narrow alley. Green blood splattered Creighdor's face.

Cold fear gripped Matt's heart. His father had shot Josiah Scanlon, Creighdor's second-in-command, at point-blank range the night *Saucy Lass* had arrived with the mummy used to replace Pasebakhaenniut. Impossibly, Scanlon had risen even though he should have been mortally wounded. Now, though, Matt knew Creighdor's head seemed somewhat vulnerable.

He took aim again, staring across the barrel of Creighdor's weapon. *One more shot*, Matt told himself grimly. At least here, face-to-face, it was not a cowardly assassin's bullet that he would use to kill Creighdor.

Gabriel moved quickly, grabbing the leather strap attached to the door and closing it just as Creighdor fired his weapon. The bullet kissed the edge of the door and went wide of the mark, striking a row of jarred tomatoes. The glass containers shattered and leaked their contents across the floor. Gabriel put the lantern on the floor and picked up a wooden slat while maintaining his hold on the door strap.

Matt fired again and again, emptying the last four rounds through the wooden door. The bullets ripped splinters from the surface and left holes he could stick his finger through. The ringing din of the detonations filled the basement.

Still on the move, Gabriel jammed the slat from a nearby broken chair through the door handle so that it wedged against the jamb. Bending, he scooped the small lantern from the floor.

"Come on!" he yelled. "Out the other doorway!" He pushed Matt to one side as a hail of bullets exploded through the door. The pale yellow light of the lantern swung crazily through the basement. "That ain't gonna stop 'em for long!"

Matt shoved his empty pistol into his coat pocket and drew his second. Then the basement door suddenly turned to kindling. Dust soared up from the floor in a great cloud. Lantern light from outside shined down on the barbaric figure that loomed in the opening.

Chapter 4

Hunched over like a fantastic beast of prey, the gargoyle was short and squat. The creature's head was broad across the bottom and pointed at the top, like someone had grabbed it by the scalp and yanked hard when it was first formed. Demonic ape features glared through the darkness, snarling slowly. Curling horns framed the head. It stood on powerful legs that ended in cloven hooves. Four arms smashed at the nearest shelves, tearing them to pieces with a horrendous clattering.

Matt stared at the creature, realizing that Paul had been right: Creighdor wouldn't enter the premises. The man didn't have to, as long as he had henchmen and beasts to call upon.

Standing his ground less than ten feet away, Matt lifted the Webley. The gargoyle must have heard him or sensed him in some manner, because the grotesque head swiveled in his direction. It lunged at him, and Matt's shot went wide, skimming off one stone shoulder instead of shattering the head as he'd intended.

Paul yanked on Matt again, and this time Matt let himself be moved. Together, he and Paul ran toward the other end of the basement where Gabriel was throwing open the door. The lantern light fell on stairs that led upward.

The gargoyle rushed toward them with inhuman speed. Matt fired twice, knocking holes in the creature's chest and hoping to damage the mysterious wiring and boxes contained within.

Seeing their plight, Gabriel stepped back and threw a shoulder into the nearest shelf. It fell over, plunging at once into the next one and setting off a chain reaction of tumbling shelves.

As Matt and Paul ran, they quickly caught up with and passed the domino effect. They had to dodge out of the way, flattening up against the wall, and were barely missed.

The gargoyle wasn't so fortunate. Halfway down the room it was caught up in the overturning shelves. The sheer weight and the momentum drove the gargoyle back and down. Four mighty fists hammered at the shelves that trapped it on the floor. Then it was free, jumping to its feet and unfurling its bat-shaped wings.

Paul took a two-handed grip on his walking stick and continued up the stairs after Gabriel. He twisted and pulled, revealing the sword blade disguised within.

Beyond the gargoyle, a knot of Creighdor's men tore free the shattered remnants of the basement door and entered. Swirling dust blunted the lantern lights.

Matt fired again. This time he took off the gargoyle's lower jaw. The monstrosity continued on, unafraid.

Creighdor's henchmen shot at Matt. Several of the bullets came close, striking the wall just above his head or by his side.

"Hold your fire!" Creighdor roared. "I'll have him alive if I can. That's the only way you'll see a bonus."

Letting out his breath, Matt took aim again and snapped off his last two shots. Both of them struck the gargoyle, shattering its left leg and sending it crashing to the floor. Unperturbed, the creature smashed its fists against the stones and swam forward.

Lunging up the steps, Matt fished cartridges from his pockets. He broke the Webley open and fed them in two by two as his father had trained him to do for quick reloads. Even as fast as he was going, with his heart pounding fiercely within his chest, he didn't drop a single round.

At the top of the stairs he followed Paul left, entering a large kitchen where a lantern burned on the stove. Two doors led from the kitchen.

Gabriel paused, deciding what to do.

A corpulent old man leaned in through the

doorway on the left. "I say, what the blasted devil is going on?"

The gargoyle reached the top of the stairs with pummeling fists.

The man turned and gasp, his mouth stretched wide with shock.

Reacting swiftly, Matt closed the Webley and pointed the weapon at the gargoyle. He squeezed the trigger and the heavy-caliber bullet smashed through the creature's head.

The gargoyle became inert at once. Sparks fizzled inside the crater in its head.

"Move!" Gabriel commanded as he shoved by the old man.

The man sagged back, crossing himself and turning pale. "A demon!" he whispered hoarsely. "God above, demons is crawlin' from the very pits of 'ell tonight!"

"Run," Paul advised, grabbing the man by the arm and shoving him into motion. "If you would live this night, run for your very life!"

"Demons!" the man said again, louder. Then he cupped his hands around his mouth and shouted. "Demons from the pits! Our final judgment is at 'and! Get up! Get up!"

Gabriel streaked up the winding stairs in the next room. Matt ran up the stairs too. Gabriel tried one of the bedroom doors on the top floor and found it locked. But the second wasn't. He opened the door and burst through, shoving the lantern into the darkness.

Matt rounded the corner at the top of the stairs. His footsteps slapped against the floor. Glass shattered ahead of him. When he reached the room he found Gabriel punching out the window with a pillow. Down floated out into the dark night and created a flurry inside the room.

"Blasted window was stuck, it was." Gabriel threw the shredded pillow aside. "Mind your step as you go now. Still got teeth 'ere." He ducked through the broken window, narrowly avoiding the broken glass shards remaining in the window frame.

Paul followed the thief after only a second's hesitation.

Matt stepped out as well, discovering that he was on a slope of roof tiles. He gazed down into the street below. One misstep would end up in a broken leg or neck.

"Come on, then." Gabriel took off at a trot, mindful of the loose tiles. Several of them slithered down the slope and shattered in the alley below.

Watchful, Matt followed. The pale moonlight made footing treacherous and deceitful. As he neared the back of the building he slipped and fell to one knee. His trousers tore, and when he stood again he felt warm blood trickling down his shin.

At the end of the building's roof Gabriel launched himself into the air. Ten feet of empty space yawned between the building they were presently on and the next. Gabriel landed easily, then turned to help.

Paul misjudged the jump and teetered precariously on the edge. Gabriel's hands shot out and caught Paul's arm, pulling him to safety.

Matt made the leap without incident. Gabriel set off again immediately. Paul followed at his heels. Bullets thudded against the rooftop and cut the wind around them.

Movement to Matt's left caught his attention. A coach recklessly plunged along the street, barely avoiding other vehicles. The driver whipped the horses with ruthless abandon. Three men with pistols hung on to the coach sides and fired again and again.

Hastening, Matt ran toward the next jump. Just as he leaped, the edge of the building he departed gave way underfoot, crumbling from old age and rot. He fell almost as much as he jumped. His arms and legs pinwheeled in the air.

With the distance barely spanned, he almost didn't catch hold of the other rooftop. Even then, he only caught hold with his free hand. When he hit the end of his arm with his full weight, he almost lost his hold. The pain was excruciating, almost enough to make him scream. He clung desperately, thinking that if he died, all chance of vengeance for his parents' deaths died with him.

Chapter 5

Dangling over the three-story drop, Matt shoved his pistol in his jacket pocket and caught hold with his other hand. Even with both arms, pulling himself up proved difficult.

The gunmen in the coach wheeled toward him, catching up easily now. Their shots closed in on him as they got the range. Pockmarks appeared in the building wall a few feet below him, then tracked up beside him.

Matt kicked against the side of the building and heaved. His arms trembled with effort and he refused to give up. Try as he might, he knew he would never reach safety in time. Gabriel and Paul had been fleeing for their lives. Even if they had seen him, there wasn't enough time for them to return and help.

Then a shadow rushed from the alley straight for the coach. Without pause, the figure intercepted one of the horses, catching the animal around the neck and shoulders. In that instant, despite the weak light of the pale moon, Matt recognized the figure because the mottled and incongruous shape could be no other. Amazement and disbelief filled him.

It was Pasebakhaenniut.

Dressed in dark and ash-encrusted rags, the mummy almost disappeared in the darkness. Pasebakhaenniut dug his feet into the cobblestones as he struggled to halt the horse, tearing several stones free and sending them shooting in all directions.

In an incredible feat of strength, the mummy lifted the horse bodily from the ground and heaved it toward its mate. Both animals went down in a tangle of harness leather.

Nothing, Matt thought incredulously, *nothing human could possibly be that strong*.

The coach rolled over on its side, spilling the driver and the gunmen. One of the men tried to regain his feet, but the mummy pummeled him with a backhanded blow that stretched him senseless.

Footsteps drummed the rooftop behind Matt. Lanterns flashed over him.

"There!" someone shouted. "There 'e is!"

The mummy looked up, his mangled face swathed in bandages that whipped like streamers around his head. "Climb, Matt Hunter," Pasebakhaenniut shouted. His words sounded hollow, like they came from deep within a dank cave.

He knows me. The thought ricocheted through Matt's mind and sent a chill slithering down his spine. *He knows my name.* The mummy had already called him by name once, which had surprised him. *If that thing truly is from ancient Egypt, how did it learn to speak English? How does it know my name?*

"Climb!" the mummy shouted.

Then Pasebakhaenniut bent and picked up one of the fallen men. With careless ease, the mummy flung the hapless man up three stories to crash into the group on the rooftops.

The screaming man landed amidst Creighdor's henchmen, scattering them. They fell like tenpins, scrabbling along the rooftop. One of them fell and screamed all the way down till he smacked into the cobblestones in the alley.

Lucius Creighdor topped the peaked roof and gazed down at Pasebakhaenniut. The mummy stared back at Creighdor, then yelled out unintelligible words.

Creighdor answered back in the same mysterious tongue, then turned to his men. "Kill it," he ordered.

Immediately, the men turned their weapons on the mummy.

Matt heaved himself on top of the roof, grateful for the distraction. He threw himself forward but paused at the next peak to glance back as Creighdor's men fired their first volley.

The mummy staggered back as several of the

bullets struck him. Bandages floated to the cobblestones. Rather than the bright green fluid that oozed from Creighdor and Scanlon, a silvery sheen spread across Pasebakhaenniut. Even as Matt watched, the silver reached its limits then began to flow back inside the mummy.

Another bullet struck the mummy's head, driving it sideways for a moment. As though angered by the bullets, Pasebakhaenniut turned and ripped a door from the coach. The mummy whirled and threw the door at the shooters.

Spinning through the air, the door smacked into the corner of the rooftop where the men stood. The impact sheared a chunk of roof from the building. A series of loud cracks signaled their doom as the roof collapsed and dragged them down into the room below.

Creighdor managed to escape the fate of his men. He took a small device from his pocket and spoke into it. Green flickers painted his sallow face.

Pasebakhaenniut turned his attention back to Matt. "Run! Run if you would live!"

Silent wings glided overhead. Matt looked up in time to see two gargoyles sail through the air. Like ravening crows, they descended upon the mummy.

Pasebakhaenniut fought the automatons at once, pounding his fists into them. Arms and legs and wings broke from the gargoyles as he battled. Their claws raked at his flesh, drawing forth the silver sheen again and again.

Three more gargoyles dropped from the sky. The mummy tried to flee, but his foes bore him down by sheer numbers. He flailed at them, but Matt believed Pasebakhaenniut wouldn't be able to get out from under their talons and jaws in time.

Settling himself, Matt drew a pistol. He braced his left arm under his right as his father had taught him, remembered painfully that his father would never again be there to teach him anything else, and took a breath.

His bullets hit two of the gargoyles, one after the other, in the head and rendered them innate. They tumbled from the mummy and shattered in the street.

Pasebakhaenniut punched through the head of another, then escaped the final two, quickly vanishing into the shadows with the gargoyles following closely behind.

Lying on his back on the sloped roof, Matt reloaded his pistol. Cautiously, he gazed back at the rooftop where Creighdor had stood.

Creighdor was gone. Only the hole in the roof remained.

Knowing there was no better time for escape, Matt gathered himself and ran along the rooftops. His mind raced as he pushed himself to cover the distance.

What was the mummy doing here? How did it find me? Or is it following Creighdor? How did Creighdor find me?

Matt didn't have any answers, but he was more convinced than ever of the importance of Cyrus Stewart's map of the mysterious shipwreck.

"Matt?"

Jerked resentfully from slumber, Matt cracked his eyes open. Harsh sunlight painted the bedroom curtains. He shaded his eyes and glanced toward the door.

He had to work to remember where he was. He and Paul changed living quarters on a regular basis, though they generally remained down in the East End these days so Gabriel's lads could watch over them.

Paul stood in the doorway.

"What is it?" Matt mumbled.

"Everyone is here," Paul replied. "Awaiting your attendance."

"Tell them I'll only be a few minutes more." Matt rolled over and tried to find sleep again. After returning last night, neither of them had easily taken to bed. Now that he had found sleep he did not want to leave its embrace.

"Matt." Paul entered the room and pulled the window shades. "They've already been waiting. You need to get up. We've just received word. Events have taken a rather troublesome turn."

Squinting against the invasion of bright sunlight, Matt saw that his friend's expression was as grave as his tone.

"What is it?" Matt asked.

Paul hesitated, obviously ill at ease. "It appears," he stated quietly, "that Lucius Creighdor has been terribly busy in the weeks that we last saw him. He outfoxed us."

"Outfoxed?"

"Very much so."

"What do you mean?"

"We've been searching for Creighdor in the crassest places. In taverns and along the docks. I'm certain he's been active there as well. But, in the end, it appears we missed his true agenda."

Matt sat up in bed. "How?"

"It's my fault, actually. I should have known better. I should have been watching."

"Paul, out with it."

"Creighdor has been soliciting support within the Queen's Court," Paul answered. "There has been some trepidation about the supply of gas throughout the city. London is still growing at a phenomenal rate. Housing, food, power—all of those things are concerns. Of late, Creighdor has concentrated considerable investments in developing the gas industry."

"He's finagled his way into the *gas* companies?"

Looking grim, Paul nodded. "That's part of it. Gas has to be made cheap to be used in the city. Pipes were laid hurriedly, trying to keep up with the demand. All of the companies were under duress to complete the tasks. The Gas Light and

Coke Company. The London. The South Metropolitan. The Phoenix. And The Commercial. All of them."

The names meant nothing to Matt. He vaguely remembered them from advertisements and from Paul's talks of Hunter Enterprises.

"I knew that Creighdor had put money into those businesses," Paul continued. "I myself had. Spreading the wealth, so to speak. Anyone with any common sense and a desire to turn a modest but dependable profit would do so."

"What has Creighdor done? Set up bombs to disable the companies and plunge London into darkness?" Such a thing, Matt supposed, wasn't impossible. The effect would be incalculable. He could never remember a time when the city had been dark throughout the night.

"No." Paul shifted uneasily. "I daresay a bomb would be much easier to deal with than what we find ourselves facing now."

"In plain English." Matt tried to keep the irritation from his voice, but that was almost impossible. His sleep had been interrupted constantly by dreams of the mummy, Creighdor, and Cyrus Stewart kicking out his life at the end of a noose under the watchful gaze of a hooded executioner.

"Creighdor has managed to start up a new company," Paul said. "The Illuminatory."

"I haven't heard of it."

"I have." Paul frowned. "I just didn't know that Lucius Creighdor owned controlling interest in it. He's kept that concealed very well. Until today."

"What happened today?"

"Queen Victoria recognized the investment made by the Illuminatory. She announced the company's value to London at a meeting of state this morning. I hear a statement to that affect is going to be prepared for release in the House of Lords as well as the House of Commons before end of week."

Matt's head throbbed from lack of sleep. His body ached from the desperate flight across the rooftops. Even now, his arm felt as though it had been yanked from its socket. "I don't understand," he said. "I see nothing in that to concern us."

Paul took in a deep breath. "As a result of Creighdor's generosity and foresightedness, the queen is bestowing a title upon him."

"A title?" Matt's head swam.

From their investigation into Lucius Creighdor, they knew that he craved nobility. For years Creighdor had been a hanger-on at court.

"Creighdor is scheduled to be titled on Friday," Paul said. "From that day forward he will be known as Lord Sanger."

A *lord*. The implications filled Matt in a dizzying rush. It was one thing to pursue Creighdor while the man was a commoner, one with ties to the city's underworld.

But as a lord, attempts on Lucius Creighdor's

life would not go unchallenged by the Crown, and his father had always prided himself on his service to the Queen. Lord Sanger. The only edge Matt had over his enemy had just been taken away. Now he would no longer be protected as a member of the House of Lords. Creighdor continued to outmaneuver him at every turn.

Chapter 6

Fresh from the bath and dressed in a clean black suit only minutes later, Matt stared at the newspaper he held in one hand. The story about Creighdor's upcoming appointment was in the lower-left front page. A photograph, taken at a recent ball, accompanied the piece.

"Lord Sanger," Matt stated bitterly. He stared hard at the murderer of his parents.

In the photograph, Creighdor stood at Queen Victoria's side and greeted well-wishers. The caption mentioned several nobles who believed Creighdor to be worthy of the title and that he would be fresh blood in the House of Lords. "A guiding force," one source called him.

"Creighdor has consistently craved power and recognition," said Narada Chaudhary, who was sitting at the table in the flat's small kitchen. He was Hindu, dark-complexioned, and dark-eyed. His dark suit was carefully appointed, bringing him instant respectability. He owned an antiquities shop and was a known expert in the field. His knowledge had been helpful throughout Matt's campaign against Creighdor. Although in his early fifties, with gray tinting his hair at the temples and sprinkling his beard, Narada was spry and quick. "That was one of the weaknesses about him that your father hoped to exploit."

"Please stop squirming," Emma Sharpe requested, tugging at Matt's tie.

Matt tossed the newspaper onto the cabinet and stood quietly while Emma finished knotting his tie. Her quick fingers tugged the reluctant fabric into place.

"There," she declared, stepping back to admire her handiwork. "You look much more presentable. I should say, my little brothers don't put up the battle you do."

"I could have seen to it," Matt grumbled.

"Later rather than sooner, I suppose. And that wouldn't do this late in the day, Lord Brockton." Emma was sixteen, trim and pretty, with strawberry blond hair, and cornflower blue eyes that glowed with a knowing innocence. Her dark green dress and matching hat showed care.

Besides Paul, Emma Sharpe was Matt's oldest friend. As a child, she had accompanied the boys on their adventures in and around Matt's family estate outside London. Matt and Paul had always been on the lookout for pirates that had come back to unearth buried treasure or American Indians seeking to scalp them. They had never found any, of course, but they had delighted in being prepared.

Emma, though she had gone with them, fording streams and skinning her knees climbing trees, had displayed different interests. Emma's attentions had been drawn to creatures and nature. Her curiosity about science still propelled her through life.

As the oldest child in her family, she helped her father as an unofficial aide-de-camp in his capacity of chief inspector at Scotland Yard. Since Matt had brought her into his confidence regarding his investigation into Lucius Creighdor, Emma's connections had proven invaluable. But even those paled by comparison to her understanding of the fantastic nature of Pasebakhaenniut and other devices and apparatus they had seen.

"Creighdor has never done anything without an ulterior motive." Matt hooked a finger into his collar and gave the tie a final adjustment.

"So you're thinkin' this gettin' titled is just Creighdor stirrin' up the dust to cover his tracks?" Jessie Quinn lounged in the open window, letting in the freezing cold because she claimed she didn't like the stifling heat trapped inside the room. She wasn't used to closed-in places, and the whole city of London was too tightly packed to suit her.

The young American stood nearly as tall as Matt. Her long, curly black hair fell loosely over her shoulders, held in place by a blue bandanna around her forehead. She looked bored. A cowboy hat rested on her bent knee.

Dressed in jeans, cowboy boots, a man's shirt, and a black duster, she looked totally out of place on London streets. However, she—like Gabriel— had the uncanny knack of disappearing in plain sight in a crowd. Perhaps she might stand out of place in Mayfair or one of the other well-to-do areas in the city, but on the docks, she didn't draw another glance.

Of course, the people down at the river didn't know about the two Colt .45 revolvers Jessie carried in tied-down holsters.

Jessie Quinn came from Austin, Texas, in the United States. Her father, Tyrel Quinn, had recently been appointed as a special trade ambassador to England, representing the interests of the western United States. The American president hoped to open up new avenues of commerce between the two countries.

Jessie was, without a doubt, the most uncommon woman Matt had ever met. Her father was a Texan, but Jessie's mother was half-Mexican and half-Chiricahua Apache Indian. She fought and rode like a man, and more competently than most men Matt knew.

"I think," Matt said in reply to her question, "that Creighdor would very much like a title and the power receiving such bestows upon him. But I also believe Creighdor has something else planned." *He's no longer simply the murderer of my parents. He's become a threat to all of England. Only no one has seen that side of Creighdor,* he thought.

"Yet he came after you last night looking for the map you recovered," said Jaijo, Narada's oldest son. He was a slightly taller, thinner version of his father, and wore glasses. He sat slightly apart from the others. Like his father, he wore a plain brown suit and vest.

"Creighdor did want the map," Matt agreed.

"Why?"

Matt looked at Jaijo. "Because of the shipwreck."

Jaijo folded his arms over his chest. "For this mysterious cargo that we can't identify."

"Us not bein' able to identify it, that's what makes it mysterious." At the stove, Gabriel plucked a hot roll from a pan and juggled it effortlessly in his hands to cool the bread. "But you can bet 'e knows, ol' Creighdor does. An' 'e prizes it some'at grandly or 'e wouldn't of come lookin' for it, now would 'e?"

Jaijo said nothing further, but he was clearly unhappy about the situation.

"I have been searching the materials I have accumulated regarding the investigation into Creighdor," Narada said, "but I have found little mention of what might have been on *Scarlet Moon* during that ill-fated voyage."

"Stewart said that there was a ship's model," Paul said. "A token or something from an Egyptian pharaoh's tomb."

"I understand that." Narada opened a small notebook. "I have all that information here in my notes, but I tell you now I have found no listing of such a thing in any of the materials I have examined."

"Then our best answer seems to be to go to the North Sea and find it." Matt approached the table and gazed down at the map they had recovered last night.

"At the bottom of the ocean?" Jessie shook her head. "Now how in blazes do you think you're gonna manage that?"

"It can be done," Emma said. "Provided you have the right equipment."

Jessie continued looking doubtful.

"According to Mr. Stewart," Emma said, "the shipwreck lies in sixty feet of water."

Matt nodded, knowing that Paul must have briefed Emma on the conversation they'd had at Newgate.

"If his estimation is correct," Emma continued, "as well as the shipwreck site, we should be able to find it."

"'We'?" Matt echoed.

Emma gave him a stern glance. "Yes."

"You're not going."

"Of course I'm going." Angry glints fired in Emma's blue eyes. "Do you really think I'd let you go traipsing off to the North Sea, near winter, by yourself?"

Defensively, Matt held his hands up. "I don't have any objection if your father has no objection." He felt safe. There was no way Edmund Sharpe would allow his daughter to risk her life in such a manner.

"My father will be none the wiser," Emma replied. "By the time you get the equipment you need, I'll have arranged everything so he will believe I'm off to France to attend a science seminar."

Although women were generally in the minority when it came to scientific studies, Edmund Sharpe humored his oldest daughter. It sometimes caused stress in the Sharpe household because Emma's mother insisted Emma become a proper young lady. Emma had a way with her father, though, and not much was denied to her when it came to her interests. Even as a child she'd been allowed to keep animals and insects—to observe them—though it had strained her mother's forbearance.

Knowing he'd been neatly outmaneuvered, Matt protested. "Emma, I can't allow you to go. Such a journey is going to be dangerous. Especially at this time of year."

"Then wait till spring."

"I can't—"

"Do you know what you can't do, Lord Brockton?"

Emma's tone was almost casual, but Matt heard the steel in her voice. He chose to remain silent.

"What you can't do," Emma went on, "is possibly comprehend what it's going to take to get down sixty feet underwater to explore the sea floor. Do you even have any idea of the equipment it's going to require?"

"There are salvagers I can talk to."

"Salvagers? Do you mean the men who dredge the bottom of the Thames River?" Emma shook her head in disbelief. "You're talking about the ocean. You're talking about several feet beyond anything the men here work. You're going to have to have specialized gear. And a ship to carry it."

"A ship is no problem," Matt said. He owned a few of them, all cargo ships that regularly traveled the trade lanes.

"Perhaps not. If you didn't have resources, you couldn't hope to do this at all. But you will need a diving suit. More than one, actually, because things can happen to a dive suit. God willing you're not in one when it does."

"I can get a dive suit." Matt had a vague memory of the brass dive helmets he'd sometimes seen aboard ships. The helmets were rare, and the men willing to descend to the ocean bottom in iron boots even rarer.

"Where?" Emma asked. "Where do you plan to acquire one? And I tell you again that one will not be enough."

"Paul will take care of that."

Looking over her shoulder, Emma glanced at Paul.

"I'll take care of it," Paul replied after a brief pause. He hated being caught in an argument between Matt and Emma.

Emma waited.

Paul shrugged. "All right. Perhaps I don't yet know how I will arrange for dive suits, but I will. I am quite capable of getting items when we need them."

Returning her attention to Matt, Emma said, "I know a man who has dive suits. We can get some from him. Renting them will be expensive."

"All right," Matt answered. "How do you know about the suits?"

"Because I've been down there." Emma glanced back at the map and stroked her chin absently.

"You've dived into the ocean?" Jessie asked.

"Yes. On three separate occasions, in fact."

Jessie shook her head. "Not me. You'd have better luck givin' a hot bath to a scalded cat than to get me in that much water."

Surprised, Matt concentrated on Emma and asked, "When did you go diving?" Her interests and experiences constantly amazed him.

"At other times when my father thought I was attending seminars," Emma answered.

"You dove?" Matt repeated. "Into the ocean?"

"The English Channel," Emma corrected. "It is a truly wondrous experience."

"Who would allow you to do such a thing?"

"A friend," Emma answered. "Someone who shares my interests in studying nature."

"What if something had happened to you?"

"Then I wouldn't be here now, I suppose." Emma remained calm and matter-of-fact. "I assure you, diving in thirty or forty feet of water is much less risky than being pursued by gargoyles."

Matt silently agreed, but he didn't think diving was that much safer. He marveled at Emma.

"You're also going to need a bathysphere," Emma stated.

"What's that?"

"A large iron ball capable of taking passengers deep within the ocean." Emma held up her hands to demonstrate the shape. "It hangs from the boom arm of a ship and is lowered into the water. Two or more people can fit inside. Depending on what size bathysphere you're able to get."

"Why would we need something like that?"

"Because even though you're having air pumped to you in a diving suit, you can't stay on the ocean floor long. A bathysphere enables you to stay underwater longer. If you're going to have to search for this wrecked ship, which is what it looks like, you'll need something that will allow you to search without getting hurt.

Preliminary searches can be done from the bathysphere with greater safety."

Matt looked at Paul.

"I wouldn't even know where to get one," Paul said.

"My friend," Emma interjected, "also has a bathysphere."

"He would be willing to allow us the use of it?" Matt asked.

"Professor Robeson has an inventive mind," Emma said. "Unfortunately, not every invention or line of exploration he conducts bears fruit. I'm sure a generous donation to his endeavors would help us, as Paul so tritely puts it, reach an accord."

"This friend," Gabriel said, "can 'e be trusted, then?"

"I walked on the ocean floor with him," Emma replied. "In the past I've trusted him with my life. Do you know anyone with a bathysphere?"

"No, miss," Gabriel responded. "Until today, I never even 'eard of one."

"Would you prefer to trust my friend? Or would you prefer a stranger who might find out Creighdor's interest in the matter and decide to butter his bread on both sides?"

Paul looked at Matt. "I vote for Emma's friend."

The others quickly agreed.

Matt sighed, not liking the situation one bit.

Every step he took toward Lucius Creighdor further enmeshed his friends in the danger that surrounded the man.

"All right," Matt said. "Paul will help arrange the donation. Let me know how quickly these things can be arranged."

A knock sounded at the door. Matt answered it, feeling a trifle hesitant—Creighdor had seemed adamant about getting the map last night.

Jessie shifted slightly and drew one of her heavy revolvers.

Chapter 7

A ragged youth stood in the hallway. "Telegram, guv. An' a note." He pushed two folded pieces of paper toward Matt.

"'Ello, Simon," Gabriel greeted. He poked his head out into the hallway. "Weren't followed, were you?"

The lad grimaced. "Course not. You taught me better than that."

"Anyone try?"

"The baroness's men. After they give me the note to bring to 'is lordship. I give 'em the slip. They thought they was good, but me, I was better."

The baroness was Baroness Csilla Erzsebet Irmuska Kardos of Budapest. She had arrived in London of late and had crossed paths with Lucius Creighdor. Creighdor had been involved in the gruesome deaths of several young girls in the baroness's country.

When she had seen Creighdor in London, the baroness had intended revenge. She had also noted Matt's own investigation into the man and had involved herself. If it hadn't been for the baroness's intervention, Gabriel would have been killed by Creighdor.

Matt had seen her upon occasion, feeling the attraction between them that had happened so unexpectedly. He stared at his name on one of the folded pieces of paper. The baroness's bold hand stood forth.

Simon wiped his nose with his sleeve. "Powerful cold out there, it is. Wouldn't mind warmin' up a little before I 'ave to go back out into it. Say, do I smell rolls?"

Gabriel let the lad into the room. "Come in. Warm up. Eat your fill."

Simon wasted no time getting to the stove. Remnants of the meal still filled platters.

Matt broke the wax seal at the bottom of the letter and quickly read the contents.

Dearest Matthew,

> *I would love to have the pleasure of your company at your earliest convenience. I miss you. It has been days since I have seen you. I would like to know how goes your private sojourn and whether I might aid you in any fashion.*

> *Yours,*
> *Csilla*

"Anything important?" Jessie asked.

Self-consciously, Matt folded the letter and put it inside his jacket. "No. A dinner invitation. Nothing more."

"Do you still keep company with her?" Emma asked.

"She does have information about Creighdor," Matt replied.

"I'd have thought, as smooth as you talk," Jessie said, "that you'd have gotten all the information the baroness has by now." Her gaze was flat, slightly mocking. "Or maybe it's not the information that interests you so much. She is a pretty woman."

"I don't believe the baroness has told me everything she knows." Matt was certain that the woman hadn't. But he couldn't deny the attraction, either. The baroness was exotic, like no other woman he'd ever met. "Creighdor was responsible for the death of her childhood friend. She would like to see him dead as surely as me."

"But she hasn't made an attempt on Creighdor's life," Emma said.

"That we know of," Matt agreed.

"Surely," Emma said, "she would have mentioned it over dinner one of the nights you were together."

Ignoring the questions and comments, Matt opened the telegram. It was from Jeremy Cothern, the journalist he'd hired to investigate

Lady Brockton's murder in Canterbury. The missive was short and to the point, stating that Cothern hadn't made any illuminating headway into his investigation regarding what happened to Matt's mother, but that he was sorting through reports he'd cajoled from the local police. Cothern promised to be in touch as soon as he had something worthwhile.

"Cothern," Matt announced. "He's still searching."

"Is he looking for the cave Kesel said Creighdor used for his experimentation?" Paul asked.

Dr. Hans Kesel was the mad physician whom Creighdor had employed to conduct fiendish experiments involving humans. Matt and his friends had tracked Kesel down and gotten only a little information the man possessed before one of Creighdor's gargoyles destroyed him.

"Yes." Matt felt slightly sick thinking of his mother's body lying on the stone floor of a cave with Kesel's cruel knives in attendance.

When Lady Brockton's body had been found by hunters, she had been carved up. At the time, no one knew why. The rumors had suggested that Roger Hunter had slain his wife in a jealous fit or while insane. Strangely, though the fact had gotten lost in the stories that were told, none of the wild animals had savaged her body while it lay there. Later, once clear of immediate charges though not of gossip, Lord Brockton laid his wife to rest in the family cemetery.

"Surely a search of real estate records in the area would have revealed something," Paul said.

"Unless Creighdor never purchased or leased property in Canterbury," Narada said. "Or, possibly, used an alias to cover his presence."

Matt turned to his friends, checking his pocket watch and finding the time to be near two o'clock in the afternoon. Cyrus Stewart had less than forty-four hours to live.

"Let's let Mr. Cothern handle his investigation for the moment," Matt said, "and focus our efforts in locating *Scarlet Moon*. How long will it take to arrange for the dive suits and the bathysphere?"

"I will send a telegram straightaway," Emma promised. "We should have an answer in a matter of hours."

"Good." Matt gathered his coat and top hat. "Let me know."

"Where are you going?" Emma asked.

"Out. I need a breath of fresh air." Matt felt immediately guilty for lying.

"Seems to me there's plenty of fresh air," Jessie stated from her position in the window.

"I want to think," Matt replied. "I think best when I'm moving." He headed for the door.

"Do you want company?" Paul asked.

"Not at the moment." Matt ducked through the door before there were any more questions.

• • •

Out on the street, Matt flagged down a hansom cab and climbed aboard, then gave an address in Regency. A quick glance out the cab assured him that Gabriel was on the move, obviously intending to follow.

When the coach rounded a corner, Matt left money on the cushioned seat and got out quickly without the driver ever noticing his departure. He hit the street running and quickly sprinted down an alley. While with Gabriel, he'd learned to find the quickest path to make a disappearance in the East End. He did so now.

Three more alleys, a trip through an underground maze where people without rented homes spent their nights, and two coach changes later, he took yet another cab to his final destination. Mayfair was one of the districts in London, unlike Cheapside and the East India Docks, where Gabriel and his lads would stick out like sore thumbs.

After paying the driver, Matt arrived at a small but elaborate dining establishment in the heart of Mayfair. Offices and personal living spaces occupied the overhead floors.

A liveried wait took Matt's hat and coat at the door. After a quick glance through the etched windows that announced simply HANDILAND'S, he crossed the floor and made his way to a private booth in the back.

Two dark-skinned men who wore foreign-cut suits sat at a small table in front of the door. They gazed at Matt with flat, dispassionate eyes. Both of them, Matt knew, were armed to the teeth and would die at a moment's notice in defense of their mistress. They barely tolerated his presence.

Baroness Csilla Erzsebet Irmuska Kardos lounged in the back of the booth. Elegant and fine-boned, the baroness still gave an impression of quiet strength even in repose. She wore a dove-gray dress that set off her chestnut hair and clung far more tightly to her than any English woman would ever allow. The style would have been daring even to the shameless French. Her gloves were of matching material and fitted her long, slender hands exactly. She was slightly older than Matt, from what he had gathered. Perhaps only a year or two, but no more than four years.

She regarded Matt with breathtaking amethyst eyes. "You came."

"Yes," Matt said. The answer was evident, but he knew she wanted him to say it aloud. It was a verbal acknowledgment of her allure.

"I didn't think you would," she said.

"Why?"

"There was the possibility that Creighdor had killed you last night."

Matt smiled. "Not yet."

The baroness returned the smile. "So I see. Bully for you." She spoke with the slightest trace of an accent.

A waiter entered the room and stood nearby, waiting to be summoned.

Matt indicated the chair. "May I join you?"

"Should I let you? After all, you ignored my last invitation."

"I did not ignore it. I didn't receive it until the next day. I came here, but—of course—you were not here."

"Perhaps."

"Perhaps I can sit?"

"Perhaps I believe you."

"It's the truth," Matt assured her.

"I'm not used to having men ignore my affections," the baroness said, breaking eye contact and looking away as though dismissing him.

"I'm not used to dealing with the affections of a woman."

Csilla laughed. "That, Lord Brockton, I do not believe at all. I've seen how those two . . . *girls* fawn after you. The chaste one as well as the American primitive."

"They are," Matt said, "my friends. Nothing more."

"If you don't see what's before your eyes, then you're a fool."

Anger stirred within Matt. For the last few weeks he'd let his infatuation with the baroness draw him to her. At the same time he knew that she could be useful in his struggle against Creighdor even though he didn't fully understand her. There was something about her that was so different from any other female he'd ever known. While running the East End with Gabriel or hobnobbing with Paul, Matt had encountered any number of young women. Csilla was the first to draw his attentions so completely.

"Should I call on you again at another time?" Matt asked. "This moment does not appear to suit either of us."

"Being petulant?"

"I'd rather prefer not being called a fool to my face."

"I've angered you."

Matt forced himself to take a deep breath. The baroness intrigued him and irritated him on a number of levels. According to Gabriel and Paul, that was the way girls rendered a man. However, he could never remember his father being vexed at his mother. Lord and Lady Brockton had eternally been in love. Matt knew he would never settle for anything less than what his parents had enjoyed.

But every time Matt looked into her eyes, part of him knew instinctively why he kept coming back. She intrigued him in a way he had never before known.

"Yes," he told her bluntly.

The baroness frowned. "That was not my intention."

Matt didn't believe her. She knew full well her effect on men. He'd watched her cross ballroom floors over the past weeks, confident of her ability to turn heads. She knew very well how she handled herself. She was very much in the society pages, and gossip flew around her.

She extended a hand to the chair on the other side of the small, ornate table. "Please, Lord Brockton. Join me."

Matt gave a slight bow and sat. "Thank you." Even as he made himself comfortable, though, he was grimly aware of the delicate deceptions *he* was playing out.

Chapter 8

Y ou'll have to forgive my jealousy," Csilla said. "I don't like a man's attentions divided when I think he should be attentive to me."

"Unfortunately, I lack the luxury of being so entirely focused," Matt said. "Lucius Creighdor, it seems, never sleeps."

"But if things were different," Csilla said softly, "do you think your interest in me would be more . . . 'focused,' as you put it?"

Matt thought about the possibility. Although he'd grown up with Emma and he admired the way Jessie comported herself, there was still something indefinable about Csilla that drew him like a moth to a flame. Though he'd felt certain that Jessie Quinn was equally as different.

In her country, Csilla had been a peasant girl who had drawn the eye of a baron. Baron Kardos had been much older than she. Within only two years, Baron Kardos had died and left the young Csilla to run his wealthy estate. Arriving in London on business, she had discovered Lucius Creighdor there and had focused on avenging her friend as well as the other young women who had been murdered.

Matt decided to answer the baroness's question as honestly as he could. "I don't know."

Csilla folded her arms and drew back into her chair. She wasn't happy. "Not exactly the answer I'd hoped for."

"It's the only one I know to give," Matt replied. "You're here on a visit. Taking care of business, you said. For the moment, Creighdor is part of that business. Once your need to remain here has been removed, would you want to live here or in Budapest?"

Csilla's gaze softened. "I don't know."

"London," Matt said, "is my home. I've traveled some. On my father's ships. I've been to France and Spain, to America, and to South Africa. I've seen a number of places, but every time I return here, to this great city, I know that I am home."

"You could visit."

"When the time was right. Now is not the time."

Csilla covered his hand with her own. "You would love Budapest."

"Possibly."

"You should let me take you there and show you what my country has to offer."

"Once I am free of my obligation," Matt said, "maybe that can be arranged."

She squeezed his hand. "I do hope so, Matt. I've grown rather fond of you."

"As I have you."

"Most men would make fools of themselves trying to get my attentions," the baroness said. "But you don't."

Matt said nothing.

"Have you ever made a fool of yourself over a girl, Lord Brockton?" she asked.

"On occasion." Matt remembered brawls in pubs over the fleeting moments spent with a saucy tavern girl.

"Who were these girls?"

"No one of consequence."

"But you were a fool over them."

"I didn't know any better. I was young."

Csilla traced his cheek with the back of her hand. Her amethyst eyes drew in his gaze. "You're still young."

"Not that much younger than you."

A trace of sadness tightened her mouth. "More than you know." She shook her head and withdrew her hand as if breaking an enchantment. "Do your friends know you're here? With me?"

"No." Matt didn't intend to ever lie to her. He knew if he did and she caught him, and he was totally convinced she would catch him, he would lose her forever.

"So you hid again," she accused.

"Yes."

"Why?"

"They are . . . uncomfortable around you." That was true, and Matt knew there was nothing to be done for it at the moment.

"Even after I helped you save your friend Gabriel?"

"Even so."

"Awfully small-minded of them, don't you think?"

"My friends," Matt replied, "have been through a lot. More than anyone has a right to expect them to go through."

"You could ask them to trust me. For your sake."

"I could. But I won't."

"Why?"

"I've asked them to trust enough on my behalf for the time." There were other reasons he didn't try to mix Csilla with his friends, though. Part of it was because he rather liked the idea of having the baroness to himself, out of the sight of the others.

"You're not here about us." Csilla sounded a little hurt.

"It is good to see you, Csilla."

She held up a hand. "But that is not the reason you accepted my invitation."

"No."

"What, then?"

"I found out something," Matt said. "A man contacted me."

"What man?"

"His name is Cyrus Stewart."

Csilla reflected for a moment. "The name means nothing to me."

"I didn't think it would. He told me about a ship that sank years ago. A ship that my father and Creighdor were interested in. A ship called *Scarlet Moon*."

Excitement widened Csilla's eyes for just a moment. "You're certain of the name?"

"I am. Do you know about the ship?"

"I've heard something of it. She was a cargo vessel. Traded in Egyptian artifacts."

"Among other things, yes." Matt nodded. He had guessed that Csilla might know of the ship. She seemed well-versed in Lucius Creighdor's affairs. "She was supposed to be carrying a model of a ship."

Csilla shook her head. Her long, chestnut locks bounced. "I don't know anything about that."

"You've made inquiries about Creighdor. Could you look for anything more substantial about the ship?"

A smile stretched Csilla's perfect lips. "I could be persuaded, Lord Brockton."

"I am here to persuade you."

"Then I shall want a ride tomorrow. Somewhere in the countryside where we can let the horses run free. And a picnic."

"I can't do it tomorrow," Matt said.

"Why?"

"Because there are preparations for Monday I must make."

"Preparations for what?"

Matt shook his head.

Csilla pouted a little. "You know I don't like it when you keep your secrets."

"I must have mine," Matt said, "just as you must have yours."

She looked at him more seriously then. "True." Quietly, she took his hand again. "Then I must insist you take that ride with me, Lord Brockton, at your earliest convenience."

"I will," Matt said.

"Let me know when you are available. I may have your information by that time." Csilla stood so abruptly, her movement caught Matt unawares.

"Csilla?" Matt stood.

"I must go," she told him. "I have my own agenda. Just as you have yours." She put her hat on her head. "Besides, I rather like keeping you guessing about what I will do." She offered her hand. "Till I see you again, Lord Brockton."

Matt took her hand and bowed. When he released her hand, she turned and walked toward the door. Her bodyguards flanked her.

Matt followed in her wake, clutching his hat. She glanced back at him from the doorway, then stepped outside and was quickly helped into a waiting coach. As he watched her leave, Matt was more certain than ever that he'd never met anyone like her. The thought made him excited and wary at the same time, which he believed to be a truly strange combination.

Early Monday morning, Matt and Paul followed the guard through the winding hallways of Newgate Prison to the great room where the hangings took place. A number of people occupied pews, talking freely among themselves.

The gallows, tall and imposing, stood with the hangman's noose dangling.

Involuntarily, Matt's stomach rolled at the thought of what he was about to witness. Regret for having agreed to be present filled him. It was one thing to watch a man fall in battle, or to take the life of another man while fighting for his own. During his campaign against Creighdor, he had done both. But this . . . this was purely cold and cruel. He stood near the wall, hoping Cyrus Stewart would see him and that it would soon be over.

A vendor offered tea and hot chocolate, making a brisk business in the crowd.

Nearly an hour passed before the court convened. The judge sat at a table with other men of station, some of them from the House of Lords, some of them from the prison. All looked sober and unforgiving.

That's as it should be, Matt supposed. *There will be no leniency today.*

After the judge was introduced, the condemned were brought forth. There were seven of them, all wearing prison uniforms and shackles, so they stood like animals at a stockyard sale.

Cyrus Stewart was the fourth man in line, standing between another man and a fat woman who wept uncontrollably. His eyes caught and held Matt's briefly, then he looked away.

"Matt," Paul whispered anxiously. "Look."

"I see him," Matt responded.

"Not Stewart," Paul said. "Nigel Kirkland."

Recognizing the name, Matt reexamined the condemned prisoners. Then he spotted a familiar face standing last in the ragged row.

Nigel Kirkland had been an unwilling pawn for Creighdor. Controlled by one of the mind parasites, he had murdered a man named Mortimer Fiske in front of witnesses. Fiske was an engineering magnate whom Creighdor had been trying to coerce into working with him.

The time hadn't been kind to Nigel. He had lost weight that he could ill afford to lose. An opium addiction and Creighdor's mind parasites had reduced him to a bag of sticks. Nigel hadn't spoken since being thrown in the sanitarium following the murder.

Now Nigel fidgeted uncontrollably. His hair

hung raggedly to his shoulders. His eyes were deep-set and hollow. Although he stood erect, he swayed a little from side to side.

"What is he doing here?" Matt demanded.

"Getting hanged, it looks like," Paul replied.

"I thought he was in an institute for the criminally insane."

"The last I heard, he was. He must have been let out these past few days. I thought the mind parasites would have done for him before now."

Unchecked by the drugs provided by Creighdor's hand-picked doctor, the mind parasites had a tendency to devour their hosts. Matt and Paul had dug up a poor unfortunate from his grave to discover that. Even while buried, the insidious creature had continued to feast on the dead man, hollowing him out.

"Creighdor must have been keeping him alive," Matt said.

"But why?" Paul's voice sounded strained. "Creighdor had already used Nigel to murder Fiske. What further possible use could he have for him?"

"I don't know."

Paul shook his head slightly. "Forgive me, but I don't know if I can watch this. Nigel was a friend for a time."

"Leave. When this is over, I'll join you."

Paul turned and started away. Then he stopped and came back. His face was drawn and haggard. "I can't. I can't leave."

After a brief preamble in which the judge was introduced and then the decisions of the court defended, the executions began. A large man wearing a black executioner's hood stepped from the guards and took the first condemned man up the scaffold. A priest followed close behind, reading from the Bible.

The man wept openly. Although given an opportunity to address his peers, he couldn't speak. He was jerked into position, the noose thrown over his head, and the lever thrown. He screamed horribly the whole time, calling out for mercy.

The screams only ended when his body hit the end of the rope. The spine shattered, and the sound rolled sickeningly throughout the room.

Below, other men took the corpse down and placed it on a litter. A physician pronounced the man dead, then the litter was carried away.

Two of the condemned tried to fight against the guards. With the shackles on their arms and legs, their efforts were doomed from the beginning.

Matt watched in hypnotized numbness. The men and the fat woman were hanged with as much emotion as wares were turned out at one of the canneries he owned. One of the men had family in attendance. An elderly woman cried out for God's mercy on the soul of her son, then she shrieked as he was hanged. Men and women surrounding her helped her from the room while others in the audience laughed and made sport of her. As each hanging progressed, runners fled to and from the execution room to keep the outside audience informed.

Then it was Cyrus Stewart's turn.

"Are you Cyrus Stewart?" the fat-jowled judge demanded, not looking up from his paper. The man seemed not interested in the slightest in those he sent to the noose. He showed neither remorse nor anticipation.

"Aye," Stewart answered in a hoarse whisper. "That I be."

"You were found guilty of the murder of your captain," the judge read from the small book in front of him.

"I was." Stewart shifted his head, holding his chin high. "I did it to save me crew."

"For your act of mutinous murder, you were sentenced to be hanged by the neck until dead."

Stewart said nothing.

"Do you wish to add anything to the record?"

"No."

The executioner took Stewart by the elbow and pulled him into position over the trapdoor. The knot of the noose was seated under his jaw, then pulled tight. The priest gave Stewart the last rites, then the lever was thrown. Stewart plunged down and his neck snapped. Only seconds later, he was pronounced dead.

Matt swallowed bile that had gathered at the back of his throat. He wanted to leave. He'd done what he'd promised for Stewart. If Nigel Kirkland hadn't been in line to be hanged, Matt would have left and tried to find some way to rid himself of the immediacy of the harsh experience that morning.

But Nigel was next.

He stood apparently without concern against the wall awaiting his appointment with the executioner. When pulled into motion, he walked steadily, though weakly, up the steps to the waiting noose.

"Nigel Kirkland," the judge called.

Standing near the noose, Nigel stared blankly at the walls.

"Nigel Kirkland," the judge repeated.

Matt looked around, thinking how callous it was of the young man's family not to at least have some representation.

One of the prison officials barked, "This is Nigel Kirkland, come before you today, your honor, to pay his just dues for the murder of Mortimer Fiske."

"Can the condemned not speak for himself?" the judge asked.

"No, your honor."

"Is he an idiot?"

"The condemned has been examined for the past month, your honor," the official said. "It was the conclusion of the attending physician that he is merely faking his condition to avoid his death."

Nigel gave no indication he'd heard anything.

Paul whispered, "Nigel hasn't spoken a word since he was sent to the sanitarium. I've tried to visit him there, and I've spoken with his physician."

"Nigel Kirkland," the judge read, "you have been judged by your peers and found guilty in the shooting death of Mortimer Fiske. Do you have any last words?"

Nigel stood and stared blankly.

"All right," the judge said to the executioner. "You may proceed."

The executioner pulled Nigel meekly along after him. Nigel appeared not to even notice. He scratched and pulled at his left ear as the executioner fitted him with the noose. Dried seepage from the ear ran down his neck. Harboring a mind parasite was not without cost even while the drugs ministered to it.

"At least in his present state he will be somewhat spared from what is about to happen," Paul whispered.

But he'll still be just as dead, Matt thought. He felt pity for the young man. Nigel Kirkland hadn't been an upstanding citizen, but he hadn't been a murderer, either. He didn't deserve death. *Neither did Cyrus Stewart.*

Paul tugged on his sleeve and, when he had Matt's attention, nodded to the back of the room.

Lucius Creighdor stood at the entrance with a matronly woman at his side. Creighdor was smartly dressed, every inch the new lord-to-be.

Chapter 9

Lucius Creighdor made his way through the audience, stopping just out of arm's reach from Matt. "Lord Brockton," he said, eyes flashing in delight. "I'd heard you were in attendance this morning."

Matt said nothing. He trembled, barely able to hold back the almost uncontrollable rage that seethed through him.

"Come to watch the festivities, did you?" Creighdor taunted. "I didn't know you indulged in this kind of entertainment. People dying after pleading uselessly for their lives. That sort of thing." His grin broadened.

Matt looked away from his mortal enemy. "I have the map, Creighdor. Whatever secrets *Scarlet Moon* possessed will be mine soon enough."

"Will they now? After being hidden for thousands of years?"

"You appear not to have given up hope of finding that ship."

Creighdor glanced at the gallows as the executioner made Nigel Kirkland ready. The young man stood as though in a daze. "Are you so conceited now that you think you know every move in our little game?"

"Pasebakhaenniut sends his regards," Matt said. He knew that Creighdor feared the mummy.

Creighdor's smile lost its smugness. His gaze cut to Matt. "You are an impertinent twit."

"The mummy hunts you," Matt said. He kept his tone conversational, as though they were discussing the weather. "Every time I see him, he's stronger. Did you know he killed Dwight and his companions not too long ago?"

Eyes narrowing, Creighdor asked, "What do you know of Dwight?"

"He was here in London," Matt said. "Presumably looking for you. Though I don't think he meant you any goodwill. He seemed to have a strong dislike of you. Granted, I was not surprised. You have a knack for making enemies of the wrong people."

Creighdor stroked his goatee thoughtfully. "You talked with Dwight?"

The only conversation Matt had had with the man had taken place over a pistol barrel. He'd been answering questions, not asking them. But he lied. He found, disturbingly, that he was getting more disciplined at that task. "Yes."

Creighdor's eyes hardened. "You play at this game, boy," he said hoarsely, "but you have not yet guessed the stakes you're playing for."

"Your life," Matt said coldly, fixing the man with his gaze. "I'll settle for that."

Creighdor chuckled. "Yet here we stand. The both of us. And you find yourself unable to act to avenge your parents."

Matt said nothing. He barely restrained his impulse to throw himself at his enemy. He regretted having left his pistols in Gabriel's keeping for the morning, but there was no way he'd have been able to bring the weapons inside the prison building.

"That's what I like about the constraints of civilization, boy," Creighdor whispered. "All those rules. Regulations. Expectations. They hamstring those of you who feel you have to conduct yourselves according to their imagined virtues. When you live according to the wishes of others, you find that you're never quite able to do everything you wish to do."

"The time will come," Matt said. "You're greedy. And, again, I know where *Scarlet Moon* rests."

The crowd grew silent as Nigel was given his Last Rites.

"Quiet now," Creighdor said. "They're about to hang poor young Nigel Kirkland."

Disgust and anger whirled in the pit of Matt's stomach. He knew he should walk away. It took all his willpower to stay away from Creighdor.

The hooded executioner tightened the noose under Nigel's jaw. The young man stood there as though nothing were happening.

"I've kept him silent, you know," Creighdor said, gazing with rapt attention. "Practically shut down his mind with my creature while he was in the sanitarium, and then here." He paused theatrically. "It would be better for Nigel Kirkland if he remained that way during the hanging, don't you think?"

A chill raced down Matt's spine as he guessed what Creighdor planned to do.

"Of course that would almost be too bloodless," Creighdor continued. "When a man meets his death, he should not be calm about it. Not calm at all." He pitched his voice lower, looking steadily at Nigel Kirkland. *"Wake."*

The command resonated in Matt's mind. He glanced at the gallows as the judge asked Nigel again if he had any last words.

As though just awakening, Nigel suddenly came to his senses. He took everything in immediately, staring at the audience before him, then at the judge seated at the table. Horror twisted his features as the realization of where he was swept over him. He glanced down, then rubbed his chin against the rope, quickly looking up to see the noose suspended from the gallows.

Nigel screamed then, a shrill sound that cut through the building. He tried to run, but the rope drew him up short, causing him to stumble and fall.

Several people in the audience laughed at him as if they were watching a clown's orchestrated antics.

"Steady, boy," the executioner growled. "Ye're only makin' it the worst on yerself." He caught the rope and yanked it back, pulling Nigel back over the trapdoor.

Insane with fear, Nigel fought desperately to keep his footing on solid ground. In the end, he failed. The executioner shoved him onto the trapdoor and pulled the lever.

Nigel's wails ended suddenly, but he'd somehow managed to work one arm free of his shackles. Maybe his emaciated condition had made his wrists too thin to be properly confined. Maybe his desperation had lent him extraordinary strength. At any rate, he grabbed the noose with one hand and tried desperately to keep from strangling.

The crowd was torn in their response. Some thought that anything less than a clean death was horrifying. Others laughed at Nigel's struggles as he kicked and fought to live.

Creighdor laughed aloud, clapping his hands in glee.

Matt started forward, unable to remain standing still any longer. The crowd was packed too tightly near the front for him to make much headway. In another moment, the executioner leaped to the floor, raced under the gallows, and took a firm grip about Nigel's feet.

For an instant, Matt believed the executioner was attempting to help Nigel. Then, before Matt even grasped what was about to happen, the hooded man pulled down on Nigel's feet with all his might.

Nigel's neck snapped like a dry twig cracking in a fireplace, loud and fierce as a pistol shot.

When the executioner released the corpse and stood, Nigel swayed drunkenly. His free hand remained trapped in the noose close to his throat.

"There now," Creighdor said, "that was more to my liking." He turned to Matt and smiled broadly.

A red haze swept over Matt's senses. Before he knew what he was doing, he leaped at Creighdor, wrapping his arms around the man and plunging them both against the press of the crowd.

Creighdor tried to escape, but Matt held him tight. Levering himself up, Matt pinned Creighdor beneath him and rained blows down on his face. The callous disregard Creighdor had held for Nigel Kirkland's life, the way he had tormented the young man at the end, built into an overwhelming frenzy. He drove his fists hard, smashing Creighdor's face.

"I'll kill you!" Matt snarled. "I'll kill you once and for all!" His voice was guttural and fierce, like the keening of a blood-maddened animal.

One of Creighdor's men grabbed Matt by the arms and yanked him away. Matt spun inside the man's embrace and hit him in the face with a clenched fist. The man's face was hard as rock. For a moment, Matt thought he'd broken his hand.

A trickle of green fluid seeped from the interloper's nose. His opponent put up a hand to hide it. He lunged at Matt with his other arm.

Wrapped in the folds of the man's jacket, Matt saw the broad-bladed hunting knife at the last second. He dodged to one side, gripped the knife hand, and butted his head into the man's face. For a moment his vision turned black and the world spun around him. He plucked the knife from the bodyguard's hand.

Gripping the knife, Matt turned on Creighdor. His enemy rose, standing on shaky legs and looking somewhat dazed.

Creighdor turned to run. Matt launched himself at Creighdor, sending them both down again. He landed on top once more, aware that men and women around him scurried away in fear for their lives. Yelps and shrieks filled the air.

"You're going to die!" Matt promised. He prepared himself for the task, yanking Creighdor around to face him. "I'm going to finish it now, you loathsome beast!"

Whatever veneer of civilized behavior had been left of him was ripped away by the emotions caused by witnessing Nigel Kirkland's and

Cyrus Stewart's deaths. He slammed his left forearm against Creighdor's head, thudding the back of his skull against the stone floor.

"Matt!"

Matt barely recognized Paul's voice. The force that drove him could scarcely be contained inside a human body. He was elemental, a power that would not be denied. He'd never felt like that before.

For months he had held his anger in check, afraid that he would strike at the wrong time and lose any chance he might have of avenging his parents. He had walked a narrow path between doing too little and doing too much.

That was over.

Matt took a fresh grip on the knife he'd taken from the bodyguard. He set the edge against Creighdor's throat.

"Can you do it?" Creighdor whispered, looking deeply into Matt's eyes. "Do you really have the nerve to take my life? Are you sure that you even can?"

Yes, Matt told himself. *You can do this. You have to. Creighdor has to be stopped.* But he remembered how he had shot Creighdor pointblank Friday night and the man had simply staggered back and shaken off the effects. *He can die.*

"Matt!"

Ignoring Paul's cries, Matt pressed the knife against Creighdor's throat. He had seen the men who were like Creighdor: men who could not possibly be men, who did not die the way other men died.

Pasebakhaenniut had yanked off Dwight's head and the man had without a doubt perished.

I can cut his head off, Matt told himself. He leaned forward, preparing to sink the knife deep. *That will kill him. That has to kill him.*

Creighdor wore a mocking grin. "Can you really do it, boy? I know your father could have. He was a warrior. Never gave up the fight. That was what got him killed at the last."

"I'll slit your throat, you unnatural beast," Matt declared. "And I'll keep sawing through your spine. You'll die."

The blade raked Creighdor's neck, drawing a thin line of green fluid. Blinding pain filled Matt's head like a mortar shell. His arms and legs went numb. Black comets swam in his vision. Unable to control himself, he toppled over onto the stone floor and lay on his back.

People surrounded him, drawing close now as the knife tumbled from his nerveless fingers. He looked up. Heaviness dragged at his eyelids. The pain throbbed more savagely inside his head. He thought his skull had been shattered and his brains must be leaking out on the floor.

Paul knelt down beside him, holding one of his hand-carved walking sticks. When Paul spoke, it sounded slow and indistinct, like it came from far across a windswept sea.

"I'm sorry, Matt." Paul's face crumbled. "Oh

God, I'm so sorry. But I couldn't let you do that. I couldn't let you kill him. Don't you see? Please forgive me."

Matt tried to get back to his feet. All he had to do was roll over and find the knife. If he moved quickly enough, he could still put an end to Creighdor. He shifted slightly, but new agony erupted inside his head and washed over him. Thick, cottony blackness filled his senses, but the memory of Creighdor's mocking smile pursued him.

Chapter 10

Agony returned first, followed by awareness. Matt lay on his back. The pressure inside his head pulsed at his ears. He took a slow, cautious breath—and when the pain hit him, he almost passed out again.

Darkness greeted him when he opened his eyes. An animal musk clogged his nose. He shifted slightly and discovered he was on a narrow bed with an iron frame and a straw mattress gone sour.

You're in jail, he told himself. He'd been there twice before while running nights with Gabriel. Caught up in a regular sweep by the bobbies, Matt had been forced to stay for hours before the thief had returned and bailed him out.

Jail made sense. After all, he had been attempting to kill Creighdor when Paul had smashed him in the back of the head with his walking stick. At least he wasn't dead.

What became of Paul? he wondered. *Is he locked up as well?*

Gingerly, Matt sat up. His head swam with the effort, and for a moment he was sure it would tumble free of his shoulders.

Braced on the edge of the narrow bed, he explored with his fingers the damage done to the back of his head. A blood-encrusted lump the size of a goose egg jutted from his skull. Even that slight touch almost made him cry out in pain.

Gradually, his eyes adjusted to the dim light coming from a lantern somewhere out in the hallway. The cell was eight feet square. Besides the bed chained to the wall, a chamber pot occupied one corner. A bucket of what Matt assumed was clean water sat next to it.

Iron bars covered the front of the cell. A locked iron-bar door with a keyhole took up one side of the wall.

Matt was surprised to find that he was still in his own clothing. Of course, he hadn't been conscious to change into the striped jail uniform. He dipped his handkerchief into the fresh water and made a compress for his aching head.

"I 'ear you over there," a male voice said. "Are you awake, then?"

"I am," Matt admitted. He tracked the voice to the front of the cell. "Where are you?"

A gnarled hand thrust out from the jail next to Matt's. "'Ere," the speaker declared. "Can you see me?"

"I can," Matt admitted.

"Thought you was a goner when they brung you in, I did. You was a frightful sight what with blood all over your face."

Matt touched his face and felt dried blood. *That explains the stiffness.* He used the compress to wipe at his face, not certain of the job he was doing. "Where are we?"

"The jail in Cheapside. Reckon you won't be stayin' 'ere for long, though."

"Why?"

"You tried to kill a man yesterday. An important man. Them bobbies, they doesn't take kindly to that, I tell you."

"Yesterday?" Matt tried to wrap his thoughts around that.

"Aye," the man said. "Yesterday. Yesterday mornin', it were. You've been sleepin' for a powerful long time. I don't think they want you dead. They let a physician in to see you. 'E said you was just gonna sleep for a while. Should wake up right as rain."

"That prognosis is certainly up for debate." A wave of dizziness almost overwhelmed Matt. His legs turned to water. Carefully, he sat on the floor with his back against the wall so he could watch through the iron bars.

"Right you are, guv. I've been walloped on the bean a few times meself. Never a pleasant experience."

"What is your name?" Matt asked.

"Tobin, milord. Bill Tobin. I'm a stevedore by trade, when I can get it."

"Well, Mr. Tobin, I wish we could have met under more pleasant circumstances."

"Aye, sir. I was fretful about you, I was. Got a couple boys about your age. I should 'ate to 'ave anything 'appen to 'em."

"Has anyone been in to see me?"

"No, sir. Onliest the guards an' their supervisor. An' the physician, course."

"My barrister hasn't been to check up on me?"

The question seemed to throw Tobin for a moment. "You got a barrister?"

"I do."

"I never laid eyes on 'im if 'e was round."

Matt considered that. The only reason he could think that Paul and the others hadn't checked up on him was because they didn't know where he was. "What are you locked up for, Mr. Tobin?"

"Drinking, mostly. Gotta make restitution at the pub where I was arrested. They tell me I tore the place up proper. Gonna 'ave a bloody big bill when I get out." Tobin sighed and spat forlornly.

"When do you get out?"

"In the morning, I suppose. Judge is makin' me sign a contract to pay for the damages."

"Are you interested in working off that debt rather quickly?"

Tobin was silent for a moment. "Course, I am."

"If you could see your way clear to get a message out for me, I'll pay that debt for you."

"What message?"

"I need to let my friends know where I am."

"Could be dangerous. That man you attacked, I bet 'e's got some powerful friends."

"Do you want to pay for that bar for years, Mr. Tobin? Debt is a most uncomfortable burden."

"The bar damages an' the court costs?"

Matt knew he wasn't going to get a better deal. His choice of messenger was limited. "All right."

"Milord, that would be awfully gracious of you." Tobin shoved his rough paw through the bars. "I'll shake on it."

Matt rose and shook hands. Then he wondered whom to send Tobin to: Paul, or Medgar Thaylor. Yet, as it turned out, Tobin knew Gabriel.

Lantern light woke Matt. He watched it dance across the wall as it came closer. He didn't get his hopes up. Other prisoners had received friends and family with the coming of the dawn. Of course, none of them had been known to him, and not one even stopped to look at him. He was simply a prisoner in the jail like many others.

"Matt," Paul called.

Slowly, Matt climbed from the bed and went to the iron bar wall.

Paul stood on the other side. He looked as

dapper as ever, but acted uncomfortable. He dismissed the guard who was with him and the man retreated.

Surveying the iron bars, Paul said, "Truthfully, I never expected it to come to this."

"Nor did I."

"They wouldn't tell us where you were. It wasn't till Gabriel talked to a Mr. Tobin that we knew for certain which jail you were in. Our inquiries were blocked at every turn."

Matt nodded and winced as the pain slammed into him again.

Leaning forward and raising the lantern, Paul inspected Matt. "How's your head?"

"Painful."

"Yes, well, sorry about that. I saw no other way to stop you. And if I had not stopped you, things would have gone much harder for you. There was every chance that Creighdor or his men would have taken advantage of the situation to kill you."

Matt leaned on the bars. "What of Creighdor?"

"You didn't cut his throat, if that's what you mean."

"You should have let me." Matt worked hard to keep the anger from his voice.

"Then come to watch you swing from the gallows for murder?" Paul grimaced. "I should think not. I've had enough of hangings, I tell you."

"I had him, Paul. I had him and would have

killed him if you had not stopped me."

"Or perhaps someone else would have stopped you and killed you while they were at it." Paul hesitated. "I'm sorry, Matt, but I truly believed I worked in your best interests. I always have and will continue to do so. You have my word on that."

"You saw what Creighdor did to poor Nigel Kirkland."

"Yes. He did it to taunt you, to push you past the breaking point. I think he wanted you to attack him."

"To what end?"

"Why, to get you out of the way, of course. Perhaps he feels a little more safe."

"There's also the matter of the Cyrus Stewart map. Creighdor wants to know the location of that shipwreck. Is the map still safe?"

"It is. We've got it in a safe place."

"Are the necessary arrangements still being made?"

"They are." Paul looked anxious. "Emma has already gotten the bathysphere and the dive suits. I've sent a ship to bring them back. It will take a few weeks to get everything in place. But those things, Matt, we can't think about those now. We need to concentrate on you."

"Why hasn't Medgar Thaylor arranged to get me out of here?"

"He's tried. He goes to court every day and talks to any magistrate who will listen to him."

Paul paused. "You don't have a lot of friends in the right places, Matt. Your father's death, all that had gone on before, has predisposed a number of people against you. Even more of those people don't know you and don't want to risk their reputations by aiding you. Especially against Creighdor when he has become one of the queen's darlings."

"When does Mr. Thaylor believe he can get me out of here?"

Paul frowned and shook his head. "He's not sure he can. You attacked Lucius Creighdor without provocation in front of dozens of witnesses."

"'Without provocation'?" Matt couldn't believe it.

"No one knows the truth," Paul said in a low voice. "If I, or anyone else, were to go before a magistrate and dare tell the story of Creighdor and the mind parasite that is doubtless eating Nigel Kirkland hollow in his grave at this moment, we would be locked up as well."

"Nigel's body will have to be tended to," Matt said when he regained his composure. "The mind parasite will have to be dealt with. We can't allow Creighdor the chance to breed those things again."

"Gabriel, Jessie, and I have already made arrangements," Paul said. "This evening, Nigel will be interred in a pauper's grave. His family wouldn't acknowledge him. Once it gets dark, we will excavate Nigel and burn his body on a pyre. The parasite will never get clear of the flames." He rubbed the back of his neck tiredly. "Of course, such a mystery as the burned corpse will give the journalists more to write about."

"What of Creighdor?"

"He's preparing to get his title tomorrow."

Breathing out, Matt forced himself to let go of the irresolute iron bars. "I've got to get out. I can't stand it in here, Paul. Being caged up like this. Like an animal."

Paul reached through the bars and squeezed his shoulder. "Chin up, Matt. We've seen bad times before. We'll get through this."

Matt didn't say anything. There wasn't enough hope left in him to speak.

Paul knelt and lifted a package he'd carried with him. "I've brought you a bag of food. I had to bribe four people to get it this far." He gestured to the guard.

The guard came over with a large key ring.

Matt summoned the last of his strength, deciding if the man opened the iron door that he was going to attempt to escape. He couldn't just sit in that dark cell and do nothing.

"Step back," the guard ordered.

Matt lifted his hands and moved back. He looked imploringly at Paul, silently asking for aid.

Paul only looked away.

The guard opened a section of the door that

Matt had not seen before, a fold-down piece that allowed him to shove the bag through. The bag dropped to the floor. With a shrug, the guard relocked the door and returned to his post.

"Your time's about up, Mr. Chadwick-Standish," the guard said with firm politeness.

Matt leaned against the bars and closed his eyes.

"Pick up the food," Paul pleaded. "You've got to keep up your strength."

Why? Matt asked himself. *What use is there? Creighdor beats us at every turn.* Discouragement spread like an infection within him. Still, it wasn't in him to completely give up. He knelt and carefully picked up the rolls, jerked meat, cheeses, and apples.

"Just a little longer," Paul promised. "Just a little longer and we'll turn it around. I give you my word."

Matt nodded. After a brief, uncomfortable silence, Paul walked away and Matt returned to his bunk. He placed the bag of food beside him, but he didn't have an appetite.

On the morning of the next day, four guards came for Matt and placed him in shackles. He fought them, but inside the small cell it was no contest. Without word, they escorted him from his cell and up three flights of stairs. With the short chain between his feet, he fell a number of times only to be hoisted up and set on his course again. The policemen cursed and cuffed him with rough hands that caused explosions of pain.

Out on the street, Matt ducked his head and squinted against the brightness. The guards took him into a narrow alley.

Medgar Thaylor stood beside a prison coach with iron bars on the windows. He looked grim and old and beaten. It was the first time Matt had ever seen him look that way.

"I'm sorry, Lord Brockton," Thaylor said in a quiet voice. "In the end, there was nothing I could do. I haven't given up trying, believe me."

The guards hustled Matt to the rear of the prison coach. One of them opened the iron door on what looked like an animal cage.

"Where is Paul?" Matt braced his feet against the coach, resisting the guards as they struggled to put him inside. "Where are my friends?"

"They couldn't be here," Thaylor said. "They didn't know when you were going to be transferred. It was all done at a moment's notice."

"Transferred?" Matt continued resisting the guards, but they roughly shoved him into the coach. He fell and sprawled. His face slammed against the rough wooden floor. As quickly as he could, despite the heaviness and constrictions of his chains, he lunged for the door.

The guards slammed the door shut in his face and placed a large padlock on it.

Matt shook the door, testing its strength. It

rattled but didn't open. "Transferred where?" he shouted.

"I could not stop them," Thaylor said. "I managed to save you from the gallows, Lord Brockton, but that is all. I'm sorry."

"Mr. Thaylor," Matt said, "where are they taking me?"

"I don't know." The old man's shoulders bowed. His eyes softened. "In lieu of hanging for the assault with intent to do murder against Lord Sanger, Judge Holcomb chose to declare you mad. You're going to a sanitarium to live out the rest of your days."

"No," Matt whispered. Images of sanitariums he'd heard about skittered through his head. Emma had talked about the operations routinely performed on those declared criminally insane: electricoshock therapy, and ice water baths that pushed patients to the point of drowning, and endless drugs—tranquilizers and purgatives. Matt had feared his father would end up there. But it wasn't his father. It was *him*.

The prison coach started with a jerk, throwing Matt's face into the iron bars. The pain echoed in the bump at the back of his head. The coppery taste of blood from a split lip tainted his mouth.

Not a sanitarium! Rooms filled with padding and shackles, where only maddened creatures kept one another company. *This can't be!*

He wanted to shout for help, hoping desperately one of Gabriel's lads might be about and could take word to someone.

Before the coach reached the end of the alley, one of the guards rushed up and slammed shut wooden doors over the iron one. No one would see him. Doubtless, over the clatter of the iron-bound wheels against the cobblestones, no one would hear him.

Numb with horror, Matt slumped to his knees and fell against the coach's side. Bars dug into his side and back as the coach jerked back and forth, but in the darkness he couldn't find it within himself to care.

Chapter 11

After his arrival at the sanitarium, Matt tried to keep track of the days. Every day the room he was in turned light, he made a mark on the wall, scratching it into the stone with his thumbnail. In the end, he realized he should have kept the count in another way, in a less obvious one.

As soon as Dr. Woodard discovered Matt's efforts, the physician had him transferred to a basement room with no windows. Then Matt tried keeping track of days by counting the breakfasts he was given. When Dr. Woodard figured that out, he changed Matt's meals to the same thing: hardtack, bacon, and water.

Then, guessing what his subject might try next, the doctor also varied Matt's meal routine. Sometimes Matt was served four or five meals in rapid succession, then hours—or perhaps days—passed with nothing to eat.

The hallway outside the iron-barred window remained lit. The guards were changed frequently, and never on any kind of routine that Matt noticed. His hair and beard grew long and shaggy, but since he'd never let either go ungroomed, he couldn't use that to mark the passage of time either.

He hoped that his friends would find him. They had been there from the beginning, most of them. He couldn't believe that they would forget about him, but as time passed, however much time that was, his hopes dimmed.

Dressed in a long nightshirt, he sat huddled in the middle of a padded room with nothing but his thoughts and fears for company. It was enough, he'd decided, to drive even the sanest person mad.

And he wondered if that was what he was there for, if driving him insane was what Creighdor's revenge against him would be. His greatest hope was that none of the mind parasites yet remained for Creighdor's use. The fear that a few mind parasites still existed kept Matt horrified all through the long hours of isolation. He thought perhaps Creighdor wouldn't use one—if he had one—out of fear of damaging Matt's mind. Then, all Creighdor wanted to know from Matt would be lost.

But, Matt knew, if that was true, Creighdor could change his mind at any time.

• • •

"Why did you attempt to kill Lord Sanger?"

Chained to a chair bolted to the floor that had proven immovable on several other occasions, Matt wearily regarded Dr. Woodard.

The doctor was in his sixties, gaunt and blunt, with gray hair and a grayish pallor. He wore thick-lensed glasses that made his pale green eyes resemble a toad's. Dressed in a white lab coat and shapeless white trousers, Dr. Woodard sat primly in his chair. He clutched a journal that he kept notes in from their talks.

"Lord Brockton," Dr. Woodard asked in his dry, unemotional tone, "can you hear me?"

"My hearing is fine."

"Then why didn't you answer me?"

"You already know the answer to that question," Matt said. "You've asked it dozens of times. You've got the answers written down in that journal. Simply look it up and read it back to yourself if you need your memory refreshed."

Dr. Woodard blinked.

During most of the consultations, as Dr. Woodard liked to call the interviews, Matt felt like a bug. Not even an interesting bug. He was just something for Dr. Woodard to poke and prod and ask questions of. None of the consultations were personal, just exercises.

"As I've told you before," Dr. Woodard said in his deadpan tone, "hostility will earn you nothing. Respond to the questions in a forthright manner and I will see to it you are placed back into the general populace of this hospital."

"General populace," Matt had discovered during the early days of his incarceration, was a large room where Dr. Woodard's victims gathered. Those forever damaged by shock treatments, chemical experimentation, and the strange operations on the brain that required cutting holes through the skull wandered endlessly till they were chased back to their cells. Most of them appeared to be flesh and blood automatons, perhaps more mindless than Creighdor's gargoyles.

Matt didn't care to visit general populace. The others in the sanitarium were grim reminders that most, if any, did not escape.

Dr. Woodard waited.

Matt waited longer. Inside, he was near to exploding, wanting desperately to break free of his bonds and try to reach the door. He made himself be still.

"You have made no progress." Dr. Woodard flipped through his notes. "I find that . . . unsatisfying."

"Think how I must feel," Matt replied sarcastically.

Dr. Woodard made a brief note. "Your father committed suicide, didn't he?"

"No."

"It is one thing to deny a parent's frailties," Dr. Woodard said. "It is a natural thing, in most cases. You do not want your parent's guilt attached to you. But if your father killed not only himself but several innocents in the process, the denial of such a thing will be all the stronger."

"My father," Matt said coldly, "did not kill himself. Nor did he kill the others in that building."

"By all accounts I've heard, you idolized your father when you were a boy."

Matt wondered where the physician had gotten those accounts. Of course, there were a number of people who had been friends to his family when he was younger. Any of those could have talked.

"Your father was fixated on Lord Sanger for his own troubles. Do you know why?"

"Because Creighdor had my mother killed in Canterbury."

"The police investigation revealed no suspects. Lord Sanger was in London at the time."

"Lies," Matt said. But he knew his answers had become automatic. He no longer felt the validity of them, and his words no longer carried weight. It was rote between them, an expected response to the physician's questions.

Dr. Woodard was silent for a moment. His stare never wavered. "Would it surprise you to know that your mother was . . . more friendly with Lord Sanger than you knew?"

"Lies!" Matt tried to stand, but the chains held him fast to the chair. Never in all of his life had he heard anything of the sort.

Calmly, Dr. Woodard reached into his journal

and took out a letter. "Would you recognize your mother's handwriting?"

Matt didn't answer. He knew his mother's handwriting. She had taught him to read and write. She had hidden maps and legends and mysterious notes in their hiding place in her greenhouse at the family estate. Several of the books he owned had personal messages from his mother.

Of course he knew his mother's handwriting.

"Is this Lady Brockton's handwriting?" Dr. Woodard held the letter out so Matt could easily see it.

The handwriting was unmistakable. It was addressed to The Honorable Lucius Creighdor, care of a London address.

Why would Mother have cause to contact Creighdor? Dazed, Matt felt as though the ground had slid beneath his feet.

For years Matt's father had never talked of what had happened to Angeline Hunter when the two of them were in Canterbury. All Matt knew was that hunters in the area had discovered his mother's eviscerated body. Later, during the few minutes they'd had together before the gargoyle had slain his father, Lord Brockton had told Matt that Josiah Scanlon, acting on Creighdor's orders, had stolen his mother away.

"Is this Lady Brockton's handwriting?" Dr. Woodard tapped the letter.

"Where did you get that?" Matt demanded.

"Your mother," Dr. Woodard said, "had a

certain intimacy with Lord Sanger that your father didn't approve of."

"No." Matt intended his reply to come out as a shout, but it was more a croak.

"Then why did Lady Brockton send this letter to Lord Sanger?" With a quiet flourish, Dr. Woodard popped open the letter so Matt could read it.

March 28, 1880

Lucius,

I have to admit to some surprise at receiving your gift today. It quite caught me off-guard.

The roses you sent are lovely, as I'm sure you know. They are taking to my greenhouse well. New buds are already forming. I eagerly await the first blossoms. You shall have to come see them when that happens. I would love to show you my greenhouse and all the joy I have discovered there.

Yours,
Angeline Hunter,
Lady Brockton

Matt closed his eyes when he finished reading the letter. Exhausted and overcome, unable to truly make sense of everything, he slumped back in the chair. "A clever forgery," he muttered.

Dr. Woodard folded the letter, placed it into the envelope, and tucked it back into the journal. "You did notice the date?"

Matt glared at the man.

"The letter was sent," Dr. Woodard said, "only weeks before Lady Brockton's murder." He paused. "Don't you agree that if you father knew his wife was exchanging such letters with a man whom he perceived to be his mortal enemy that he would be unhappy?"

That didn't happen, Matt told himself.

"If Scotland Yard had seen this letter, and others like it," Dr. Woodard went on, "I think their investigation into your father's and Lady Brockton's murder would have been much more conclusive."

"No," Matt uttered.

"Do you know what I think?" Dr. Woodard leaned forward in his chair and put his face close to Matt's. "I think your father took Lady Brockton to Canterbury for the sole purpose of murdering her for her indiscretions."

Fury gripped Matt. He braced his feet against the floor and shoved for all he was worth. The chains cut into his chest. Still, he refused to give in, shoving harder and harder.

With loud snaps, the front legs of the chair tore free of the stone floor. Matt tipped over backward. As soon as he landed, he threw himself violently from side to side. Another brace snapped. The chains over his chest and arms loosened as the chair came apart.

Hurriedly, Dr. Woodard drew back. He called for an orderly.

Two burly men in white uniforms burst into the room.

Shaking free of the chains, Matt tried to get to his feet. Even as he rose, the two men hammered him back and down, taking him to the floor. He fought, kicking and punching, even trying to bite.

One of the men put a hand on Matt's face and shoved his head back. His skull bounced off the floor, and pain flashed through his head. The injury he'd received from Paul's walking stick hadn't healed completely.

"Hold him," Dr. Woodard said.

Unable to fight free, Matt watched in horror as the physician approached him with a long, metal hypodermic. Dr. Woodard plunged the needle into Matt's neck. A burning hot flame raced through his veins, straight up his neck into his head. His brain exploded, and he went blind and deaf.

Madness pressed in at Matt as the drug ran its course. Nightmares and hallucinations twisted memories of his mother and father. Sometimes Matt witnessed his father killing his mother. Other times, Matt envisioned Lady Brockton in Lucius Creighdor's arms. Matt tried to deny them all, but they persisted, torturing him in ways he had never before known.

His mother was the kindest, gentlest person he had ever known. But he had been a child when he had known her. A child didn't know everything that went on in the adult world. He *still* didn't know a lot.

So far during Matt's incarceration, Dr. Woodard hadn't subjected him to electrical shocks, ice baths, or drugs. Matt wasn't sure why. Those options seemed to be the physician's favorites.

Later, though he didn't know how much later, Matt woke up in his darkened room. He was steeped in sweat and chilled to the bone. His teeth chattered. Pain pounded fiercely inside his head. Again and again he threw up into the chamber pot, inhaling the sick smell so that he threw up again.

After a while, mercifully, sleep claimed him once again.

When he woke up, Creighdor was in his room.

"Good morning, Lord Brockton," Creighdor greeted casually. "Or is it evening? I forget." He sat in a chair, knees crossed and looking rested. "I've found, in my long life, that time is vastly overrated. But you've not had much use for time lately, have you?"

Arms trembling with effort, Matt pushed himself up. He intended to get to his feet but failed. He settled for putting the wall to his back.

Two menacing men stood on either side of the door behind Creighdor.

"Have you enjoyed your stay here, Lord Brockton?"

"What do you want?" Matt could barely make the words come out. Whatever the drug had been that Dr. Woodard had given him had been extremely potent.

Creighdor smiled. "I want *Scarlet Moon*."

Matt leaned back, resting his injured head against the wall. The painful contact was enough to send color bouncing through his mind. "No."

Snorting in displeasure, Creighdor said, "Come, come. You've made a brave show of it while you've been here. But enough is enough. I've exhausted my patience."

"I've not yet exhausted my endurance," Matt croaked.

Creighdor's face hardened. "Then you're a fool, boy. I want the map that Cyrus Stewart left you."

"I'll die before I give you that map."

Leaning back in the chair, Creighdor nodded and smiled. "Well, we'll see if you truly mean that, I suppose." He stood and gestured to the men.

Matt wanted to fight. He at least wanted to try to escape. But he couldn't move.

The men grabbed him under the arms and lifted him to his feet. When he wasn't able to walk, they dragged him after Creighdor out into the hallway.

Dr. Woodard followed. "Lord Sanger, I only just learned you were here."

"Hello, Doctor," Creighdor greeted him.

Confused, Dr. Woodard fell into step with

Creighdor. "What—what are you doing with my patient?"

"I'm treating him," Creighdor answered. "Something you failed to properly do."

"But, sir, I did all I could within the parameters you set. It was you who did not want to employ the drugs or the other methods I have at my disposal."

Creighdor took a left turn and went up a long, winding flight of stone stairs. He plucked a lantern from the wall and used it to chase back the darkness that filled the hallway.

"I did not want to risk damaging his mind, Dr. Woodard," Creighdor snapped. "I've seen some of the horrors you've unleashed upon your patients."

"I didn't harm him."

"You also didn't break him as I'd requested." Creighdor paused at the bottom of the stairs and held up the lantern to shine over a metal door. He rapped impatiently on it. "Open it, Doctor. Let's get to your little chamber of horrors, shall we?"

Woodard fumbled in his pocket and produced a heavy key ring. Fitting a key in the lock, he twisted and pushed open the door.

Creighdor went through, holding the lantern out to illuminate the room.

Chapter 12

"Chamber of horrors" was an apt description, Matt decided as he gazed over the room's contents. Chains and leather bindings hung on built-in racks. Bloodstained straitjackets shared space with iron rods and bars. Manacles hung from the walls near generators. Two huge tubs sat on either side of a wooden chair bolted to the floor.

A window occupied one wall. Moonlight glinted on the iron bars set in stone. It was night outside. Matt took some small comfort in finally knowing what time of day it was. Off in the distance, lightning flickered. A moment later, thunder boomed.

The two men forced Matt into the chair and tied him with leather restraints. One crossed to a large generator and started it up. The deep *pop-pop-pop* of the engine filled the room, and vibrations shuddered through the floor.

Surprisingly, Matt found little fear in himself. He knew it wasn't because he was brave. Rather, he was empty of fear. Out of habit, he pulled at the restraints, searching for some sign of weakness, not finding any.

Creighdor put his top hat on a nearby metal table. He placed his hands on Matt's arms and leaned down into Matt's face.

"I tire of you, Matt Hunter," Creighdor declared. "You've been a thorn in my side. For a while I let you live so that you might guide me to the secrets your father kept. Now that I look back on it, I would have been better served if I'd simply killed you outright alongside your father."

"Then do it," Matt whispered.

Creighdor glared at him. "Don't tempt me, boy. Killing you would be easy. Trust me on this: One way or another, you're going to die tonight. It's up to you whether you depart this life quickly or die by inches."

Matt said nothing, but the sour taste of bile clung to the back of his throat.

"I want to know the location of that shipwreck," Creighdor said.

"I don't have the map."

"No, but you have seen the map. You can reproduce it."

"I won't."

With blinding speed, Creighdor slapped Matt. The blow landed hard enough to turn Matt's head. For a moment he thought he was going to pass out from the pain. When he turned back to face Creighdor, Matt spat blood in the man's face.

Outside the window, lightning blazed again. This time the thunder sounded louder, on the heels of the lightning now. The storm was gathering strength and growing closer.

"You're a fool, Matt Hunter! All you've got left is your pride! Do you really think you can take that to the grave with you?"

"I will. And my honor."

"Pride and honor! Bah!" A crazed look filled Creighdor's face. "Do you know what really makes this world or any other spin round, boy? Do you?"

Matt didn't answer.

"Power," Creighdor answered. "Power and wealth. Those are what every man answers to. No matter where you go, no matter how far, those remain the two constants."

"You're demented," Matt said.

Creighdor backhanded Matt. Matt's head rocked back, and his vision dimmed for a brief moment.

"I have struggled and fought, warred and killed," Creighdor roared, "for thousands of years. Against enemies whose names I can't even remember. I will not be stopped. You need to understand that. I will not be stopped by you or by any other. *Ever!*"

"You haven't got *Scarlet Moon,*" Matt said.

Everything in him cried out to battle, to beat down the man who had destroyed and murdered his parents. Even at the last, Creighdor had tried to take away Matt's memories of his mother, had forced him to question once again his father's sanity.

Creighdor blew out a big breath. "We're alike, you and I. More so than you know. Your mother, in a sense, birthed both of us."

Confusion filled Matt.

Grinning, Creighdor said, "See. You don't know everything. Not even as much as you'd like to know. Nowhere near enough to be a threat to me, at this point."

"What are you talking about?" Matt asked.

"Tell me the whereabouts of *Scarlet Moon* and I'll tell you how your mother came to be down in Canterbury."

"She went with my father," Matt said hoarsely. "To spy on you."

Creighdor laughed. "No. She came to see me. Dr. Woodard has shown you the letter she wrote to me."

"You're a liar!" Matt snarled.

"No," Creighdor said. "I'm not. Not about this. In this, the truth will hurt you more than any lie I might weave." From a black medical bag on the table, he picked up a long piece of metal that looked like a knitting needle. "Do you know the nature of Dr. Woodard's brain surgeries, boy?"

Coming close, Creighdor poked the device within inches of Matt's left eye. "I find Dr. Woodard and his work here fascinating," Creighdor stated. "Over the years of our association he's told me about an Irishman named Phineas Gage, a mine worker who suffered a tragic accident that left a metal rod thrust through his face and brain. When surgeons removed the rod and Gage somehow lived, they discovered his personality had changed."

Dr. Woodard smiled a little. He stood nearby, with his hands clasped behind him. "A most interesting case, I must admit. I deduced that the personality is housed in the frontal lobes of a person's brain, as did many of my colleagues." He touched himself between the eyes. "Only an inch and a half back behind the eyes. However, I am one of the few who has scientifically searched for the truth of the matter."

"He's been operating on some of the more violent patients in his care," Creighdor said.

Matt remembered the men and women he'd seen with unexplained scars on their heads and faces. He'd been told that Dr. Woodard had performed some type of new brain surgery.

"At first I cut open the skulls of those patients," Dr. Woodard explained. "Then, once I had performed the operation a few dozen times, I learned that I don't have to perforate the skull and risk massive infection to the brain."

"No," Creighdor said. "The good doctor simply rams a needle—*this* needle—in through the eye and cuts through the frontal lobes." He traced the needle down Matt's cheek. "Now the procedure can be done in minutes. Dr. Woodard assures me that once you've been reduced to that state, you'll answer any question I put to you."

Sickness—and a new fear—roiled in Matt's stomach. He struggled against the restraints and the men again but didn't manage to loosen either the bands or the men's grip on him. He was trapped.

"Unfortunately," Creighdor went on, "the possibility remains that you will suffer a complete loss of awareness. Like some of the patients you've seen."

Matt remembered those people. They'd been shambling shadows, drifting and aimless in the halls, sometimes stopping at walls and standing there for hours until their legs gave out. He didn't want to be like that. He *couldn't* end up like that. Surely it was worse than dying.

"So," Creighdor said softly, "my question to you becomes whether you want to risk becoming a mindless vegetable or whether you will draw the map for me."

Matt wanted to say *no*, but he couldn't find his voice. His breath rasped through his mouth and nose as fear ran rampant through him.

"You're stubborn, boy," Creighdor said, "I'll grant you that. Your friends have all been clever in your absence. I've not been able to catch any of them unawares since you've been away. Nor have I been successful in managing an exchange: you for the map." He shook his head. "They believe you are dead." He shrugged. "I could take you to London, of course, show them that you still live, but I don't relish taking the chance of letting them somehow spirit you away. Or being forced to possibly kill them all and end up with nothing for my trouble."

Thunder boomed in the room, louder than the generator. Matt shuddered against the cold steel needle pressed against his face.

"So, you see, I can have Dr. Woodard perform his miraculous operation," Creighdor said, "and I can still take you back to London and secure a trade with your friends—you for the map."

Matt closed his eyes.

Creighdor came close and whispered in Matt's ear: "Now, Lord Brockton, tell me how you will answer me."

"I will not aid you," Matt said, his breath getting harder to take with each word.

"Dr. Woodard." Creighdor backed away with a harsh oath, folding his arms over his chest in angry disgust. "Minister to your latest patient. I shall await the results of your gifted touch."

Looking animated for the first time, Dr. Woodard plucked the slim needle from Creighdor's hand. "Do you want me to give him anesthesia?"

"No."

"As you wish." Dr. Woodard leaned forward and placed the tip of the needle at the corner of Matt's left eye.

Overcome with helpless rage, Matt closed his eyes. The sensation of the needle pressing against his flesh made him violently ill. He tried to keep his eyes tightly closed, but Dr. Woodard placed a thumb on his left eye, opening it.

"You must look at me," the physician commanded. "If I err, you will be blind in that eye."

What will it matter? Matt wondered.

Another flash of lightning lit up the room. In the harsh glare across the room, Matt saw the horrid face of the incredible being through the iron bars of the window.

"Pasebakhaenniut," Matt gasped.

At the mention of the mummy's name, Creighdor spun to face the window. He unlimbered a long-barreled pistol from inside his jacket.

The mummy shifted at the window and shouted something in the arcane language Matt didn't understand. The words sounded too harsh and grating to be made by a human throat.

Creighdor shouted back at Pasebakhaenniut, then fired. Inside the room, the gunshot cracked nearly loud enough to rupture the eardrums.

Chapter 13

Startled by the exchange and the gunshot, Dr. Woodard whirled around. The needle dropped from Matt's eye.

Pasebakhaenniut jerked back from the force of the bullet that struck his cheek. The decayed flesh and bandages tore at the side of his face, exploding outward. Then the silvery liquid rushed forth to cover the gaping wound that would have surely killed anything mortal.

Growling inarticulately, the mummy caught hold of the iron bars and pulled. He hauled himself up so that his feet were braced on either side of the window. Stone and mortar cracked as he pulled the bars from the wall.

Creighdor broke open his empty weapon and struggled to reload. He snarled commands in the unknown tongue to the men who had accompanied him.

Pasebakhaenniut yanked the bars free, leaving a hole in the wall. He caught hold of the floor as he fell and stopped his descent.

The two men rushed across the room. They fired pistols at the mummy, but most of the bullets went wide. The others seemed to inflict no harm. Out of bullets, one of the men stomped at the mummy's head and hands, seeking to dislodge him.

Moving with incredible quickness, Pasebakhaenniut caught the man's foot and yanked him through the hole in the wall. The man's hoarse scream faded as he dropped.

The other man grabbed a set of manacles and whirled them over his head. When Pasebakhaenniut hauled himself into the room, the man hammered the mummy with the lengths of chain. Bandages ripped and flew.

Matt struggled, but couldn't get free of the chair. He watched helplessly as Creighdor fled the room and vanished.

"He's getting away!" Matt shouted. "Creighdor's getting away!"

Creighdor's man kept fighting, his moves graceful, like some of the Chinese warriors Matt had seen in Shanghai when he had gone there on his father's ship.

As graceful as the man was, though, his unnatural opponent was even better. A flurry of exchanged blows, almost too quick for Matt to keep track of, knocked the man back. In the next instant, Pasebakhaenniut had his huge hands on the man's head and viciously twisted.

Torn from its moorings by Pasebakhaenniut's brute force, the man's head came free of his shoulders with a terrible wrenching sound. Instead of blood, virulent green light exploded from the headless corpse. Even as the dead man dropped toward the floor, his body—including the head in Pasebakhaenniut's grip—turned to green light and vanished.

Dr. Woodard backed away, staring at the incredible apparition before him. "No! Stay away!"

Pasebakhaenniut pounced on him. Spinning, the mummy heaved the physician through the hole in the wall. Dr. Woodard didn't start screaming till after he'd started his fatal fall. Thunder swallowed up the sound.

Turning his attention to Matt, Pasebakhaenniut crossed the room.

"Are you . . . all right?" the mummy asked.

"I am," Matt replied, although he felt he could scarcely stand on his own. "Creighdor is escaping."

"He will . . . return. He has . . . more weapons . . . outside. More . . . men." Pasebakhaenniut regarded Matt with true eyes instead of the hollows that had been there. "I have . . . to get you . . . out of here."

Close up to the mummy, Matt saw that the changes that had been taking place the last time he had seen Pasebakhaenniut had progressed. He wore pants, a shirt, and a long jacket, but only bandages covered his hands and feet and face. More flesh showed underneath the bandages, but it was raw and reddish, like blood blisters. Musculature showed in sharp relief.

Most incredible of all was the network of metal that ran the length of the mummy's limbs. The metal rods were jointed and fitted together as intricately as the gears in a Swiss watch. They moved and flashed as Pasebakhaenniut tore the leather restraining straps and the chains from Matt. Under the hood, more of the metal wrapped the mummy's head, knitting a spiderweb over the back of his skull.

"Why are you here?" Matt asked.

"I . . . came to . . . rescue you."

"Why?"

"You are . . . Creighdor's enemy. You are . . . innocent. It is . . . what I do."

"What you do?" Matt struggled to comprehend. "I don't understand."

"You . . . don't have to . . . understand, Matt Hunter. You only . . . need to escape. Can . . . you walk?"

"Barely." Freed of the restraints, Matt stood. His legs felt weak and wobbly. He still suffered the effects of whatever drug Dr. Woodard had given him. "How did you find me?"

A rictus pulled at the mummy's face. The expression was the stuff of nightmares. "I . . . followed Creighdor. I knew . . . that he would have . . . to come here . . . eventually."

Someone shouted out in the hall. The pounding of running feet came closer.

"Hurry," the mummy urged.

"There's only one way out," Matt said. "There were no hallways along the corridor that I saw."

Swiveling his massive head, the mummy looked at the hole in the wall. Driving rain glistened silver in the moonlight. Cold filled the room. If it were only a little colder, Matt knew, it would be snow instead of rain.

"There is . . . a way." Pasebakhaenniut approached the opening.

Joining the mummy, Matt peered down. Although he had seen little of the asylum upon his arrival, he'd seen enough to know that the structure had been situated in mountainous terrain. He had guessed that they were somewhere north of London, around Ipswich.

What hadn't been revealed was that the asylum backed a sheer cliff with a three-hundred-foot drop. Lightning sizzled, bringing out the craggy surface of the nearly vertical cliff. At the bottom, a narrow river cascaded over broken rocks. Forest spread out in all directions. Then it was dark again.

"We must . . . climb," Pasebakhaenniut said.

Reluctantly, Matt crawled through the opening and began his descent. He was thankful there were several cracks and crevices in the stone face. He jammed his fingers and bare toes into them and started down.

The sharp edges of the rock cut into his hands

and feet. Blood seeped from the wounds and made his grip and footing tricky. The cold wind slammed against him, driving the freezing rain harder. In the space of a drawn breath, the flimsy nightshirt was drenched and plastered against his skin. His soaked hair lay in his face and dripped water into his eyes.

"Faster," the mummy commanded.

Matt didn't argue. He went as fast as he could, certain that he would make a misstep that would send him plunging to his doom.

Pasebakhaenniut moved along the cliff side with the easy grace of a spider. The metal rods on his arms and legs functioned smoothly, rhythmically.

They had only traversed thirty feet, perhaps less, when Matt heard Creighdor's voice above. Matt looked up before he could stop himself, knowing he was wasting time.

Creighdor stood in the opening. The wind whipped his hair into a frenzy. Lightning lifted his sallow features from the darkness and turned them bone-white. Madness gleamed in his black eyes. Turning, he took a strange, glistening tube from one of his men. He placed the device on his shoulder and leaned out farther, taking deliberate aim.

Then, a bright green beam, like the one from the gargoyle's eyes that had killed his father, flashed by Matt's face. The heat of the beam was almost enough to sear his flesh.

Starting his descent again, crawling as quickly as he was able, Matt knew they would never make it. Creighdor would soon have the range. They had too far to go.

"Matt Hunter," Pasebakhaenniut called.

Hoping for some miracle, that perhaps the mummy knew of a cave he had missed in the darkness, Matt glanced up. Driving rain slashed into his eyes, blinding him.

Creighdor's weapon fired again. The beam struck the cliff side only a few feet away. The stone turned red-hot and puddled, running like candle wax. The acrid stench of burning rock filled Matt's nose.

At least it will be quick, Matt told himself grimly.

Scuttling above him, Pasebakhaenniut suddenly let go of the cliff and dropped. He caught Matt, knocked him from the cliff, and wrapped him in his giant arms.

They fell just as Creighdor's next shot hit the area where they had been.

Instinctive fear and horror ripped through Matt. Over two hundred feet remained to fall. He struggled to get away, but the mummy held him tight. All Matt could think about were the rocks waiting at the bottom of the drop. The mummy had sent them both to their doom.

Then water closed in over him, filling his eyes, nose, and mouth.

The river! Matt realized. The long fall pulled them deep, then the current drew them.

A beam of green light stabbed into the river. The water boiled, and a great steam cloud rose from the water's surface, obscuring the view of the cliff and the asylum perched atop it. Two more beams struck, but the current carried Matt and the mummy farther downriver.

Matt tried to fight free of the mummy's grip, certain he was going to drown before Pasebakhaenniut realized he had to breathe, but he wasn't strong enough. The mummy swam with one arm, angling out of the strong current.

Deep in the murky water, Matt couldn't see anything. From above, the river hadn't looked especially deep. They bounced off of rocks and rough surfaces. Then the mummy found his footing. Pasebakhaenniut slipped and fell half a dozen times before successfully standing.

Just when Matt knew he could hold his breath no longer, his unnatural rescuer carried them free of the river. Gasping, not believing he was still alive, Matt sucked in air. Then the cold set in, wracking his body with shivering that palsied his muscles. He could barely move his eyes. His vision blurred.

They had come out of the water at least a thousand yards downriver from the asylum. Green light shot out from the structure crowning the cliff, striking the river at the bottom again and again.

Finally, it stopped.

Shivering uncontrollably, Matt lay helpless in

the mummy's arms. He couldn't feel his body. He was convinced each breath he drew would be his last.

Pasebakhaenniut moved through the brush, cradling Matt as though he were a babe in arms. Without warning, the green light flashed again, striking a nearby tree and turning it to ash. The beam left a smoking crater the size of a hansom cab burned into the earth.

"He has . . . a range finder," the mummy said. "I didn't . . . expect that. He has salvaged . . . more equipment . . . than I had . . . believed."

Another beam burned into the forest ahead of them and toppled trees. More smoking craters opened in the earth like burst pustules.

Effortlessly, Pasebakhaenniut ran. He took an evasive course, dodging through the brush and the leafless trees.

Overcome by the cold, Matt passed out.

Chapter 14

Warmth drew Matt back to consciousness from a nightmare. In the dream, he'd been trapped in a cavern, frozen in ice, and was watching helplessly as the opening slowly iced over. Returning to a wakeful state after all he'd been through didn't promise any better circumstances.

Pain radiated throughout his body. Opening his eyes took nearly all his strength. Soft orange light glowed all around him and created a canopy overhead. He lay on the ground. Cautiously, afraid it would snap off, he turned his head and looked for the source of light.

A puddle of molten rock sat in a hollow depression in a stone floor. The rock seethed and rolled restlessly, like a live thing trying to escape the confines of its prison.

He was in a low-ceilinged cave. Warmth filled the space, and he luxuriated in it. His body still felt cold and was knotted up from shivering. Realizing a heavy weight pressed down on him, he looked and found a bearskin covering him.

"Can you . . . eat?" the mummy asked in his distorted voice.

Glancing across the molten rocks, Matt made out the dim outline of the mummy sitting cross-legged in the darkness. Pasebakhaenniut's eyes glowed with incandescence.

Hunger gnawed at Matt's stomach, surprising him. "Am I alive?"

"It would . . . appear so. Yes."

"Where's Creighdor?"

"Gone."

"He left the asylum?"

"Yes. His men . . . searched for us . . . for more than a day. I kept us . . . hidden."

"A day?" Matt couldn't believe so much time had passed. It wasn't until a moment later that he thought to be surprised the mummy had successfully hidden them for a whole day.

"Yes. You were . . . very ill." The mummy shifted slightly, adjusting the long jacket he wore. "Your body is . . . vulnerable to . . . a lot of things."

Matt studied the mummy. "How did you survive?"

"I . . . outran them. I . . . am more skilled . . . at hiding . . . than they are . . . at looking." Pasebakhaenniut worked his jaw deliberately, as if answering all the questions brought him pain.

"Not now," Matt said. "How did you survive after being dead for thousands of years?"

"I was . . . not dead. Not . . . as you understand . . . death."

"Your body was decayed."

"True."

"You were not alive."

"No. But I was not . . . dead."

"How?" Matt knew that Emma would have a thousand questions. He felt like an idiot because he kept repeating the same one over and over.

"I have . . . a survival system," Pasebakhaenniut said. "Unless it . . . too is . . . destroyed, I . . . will survive." He stretched out a hand. "Injuries are . . . repaired."

Repaired? Not healed? The strange answers fascinated Matt.

The soft glow of the light revealed that Pasebakhaenniut was missing the last three fingers on his hand. Stumps of bone stuck out amid torn flesh. "I was . . . injured in . . . the river. My hand."

The silvery liquid Matt had seen before poured out. Before his eyes the fluid created three outlines of fingers, then quickly began filling them in.

"What is that?"

"They," the mummy replied. "They are . . . surgeon automatons. Apparatus that . . . functions independently. That is . . . the closest I can . . . describe them . . . in your limited language. If I had not . . . diverted energy . . . to save you, my hand . . . would already . . . be rebuilt."

Gazing closer, Matt saw that the fluid was indeed comprised of thousands of tiny silver beads. "My 'limited language'? Where are you from?"

The rictus pulled at the mummy's mangled mouth again. "Far . . . far away." He replaced his hand back within his robe. The light from the rocks reflected from the silvery sheen on his face. His features looked closer to human now, and the wound caused by Creighdor's bullet looked like it had torn through flesh and blood. Except that the wounds were closing.

"And Creighdor? Is he from there too?"

"No." Pasebakhaenniut shook his head and made the bandages flutter. "The one . . . you know as . . . Creighdor is . . . from somewhere other than the place I am from."

"Where?"

"You would not . . . understand . . . or believe. Your . . . comprehension . . . of . . . what is out there . . . is too . . . limited."

"Try."

"No. I will not . . . speak of . . . those matters. I am programmed . . . not to divulge . . . information." Pasebakhaenniut looked at him. "Can you . . . eat? You need . . . your strength. I was . . . only able to . . . mend you in . . . a limited fashion." He plucked a raw piece of meat from a pile beside him and tossed it onto the molten rock.

The meat began to cook, and the smell made Matt's mouth water. The whole time he had been incarcerated in the asylum he'd never gotten anything more than weevil-filled bread and thin, soupy gruel.

"Why did you come after me?" Matt asked.

"It is . . . what I am . . . supposed to do."

"Rescue me? That's what you're supposed to do?"

Pasebakhaenniut appeared to rethink his answer. "I . . . protect. I am . . . a Protector." He flipped the meat onto the other side.

Just from the way the mummy answered, Matt knew that *Protector* was a title. "A Protector of what?"

"Innocents."

"How did you become a Protector?"

"That is . . . the function . . . I was crafted for."

Matt struggled hard to grasp what the mummy was saying. He failed. It was too much. "Crafted? How?"

Pasebakhaenniut took the seared chunk of meat from the molten rocks. "Too much talk. Eat."

With difficulty, Matt sat up. His hand shook as he took the meat from the mummy. He didn't believe for a moment that his reaction was entirely from the physical hardships he'd suffered through.

He chewed the meat, finding it laden with fat and unadorned by any spices. Still, it was rich and good. He wolfed it down.

"Where did you get the meat?" Matt asked.

"The bear."

"What bear?"

Pasebakhaenniut gestured to the bearskin wrapped over Matt. "That . . . bear."

Glancing down at the fur, Matt said, "Oh." He hadn't stopped to wonder where Pasebakhaenniut had gotten a bearskin in the middle of the forest. He took another bite. It was like venison or wild rabbit, with a strong gamy taste. "I've never eaten bear before. Does it agree with you?"

"Not while," Pasebakhaenniut said, "it was alive."

"Is Creighdor like you?" Matt stood outside the cave and looked around. First morning light stained the eastern sky purple and pink.

Snow had fallen during the night, blanketing the area in pristine white. The bare branches of the trees and bushes stabbed toward the dull leaden gray sky. Icicles hung from some of the limbs. A quiet wind stirred the snow.

"No," Pasebakhaenniut answered.

Matt pulled the bearskin around him more tightly. During one of the times he had slept, the mummy had fashioned boots, leggings, and a coat and sewn them together using a bone needle and sinew for thread. There was even a cap to keep Matt's head warm.

"Creighdor's not like me," Matt said.

"No." Pasebakhaenniut surveyed the country-side.

A pile of white bones—bear bones, Matt assumed—sat in front of the cave. "Can Creighdor be killed?"

Pasebakhaenniut looked at him. "Yes."

"Good," Matt said, then he started southwest, toward London, putting his face into the wind and the swirling snow. It was a long way back. He felt strong now, though. The rest and Pasebakhaenniut's ministrations had proven rehabilitative to an extraordinary degree. "Then you must tell me how."

Hours later, they found an old road leading through the forest. It was hardscrabble, a swath that had been cut through trees and brush by stubborn men and necessary trips. Coaches didn't travel that way often, but they did come by. Matt knew that from the deep ruts cut in the earth that even the snow hadn't managed to completely cover. In addition, he stumbled through a few of those ruts a time or two.

Pasebakhaenniut didn't speak much. Matt's mind stayed occupied with all that he had learned. During the long walk, the mummy continued to heal. His hand was nearly whole now, his fingers filled in, and his face wasn't quite as terrifying. Scars showed at the side of his face instead of gaping wounds.

"Why didn't you protect others Creighdor has killed?" Matt asked.

"I have . . . tried." Pasebakhaenniut looked around, watching geese flying south in a V formation. "In this place . . . in this time . . . Creighdor has become . . . very powerful. He has . . . an army. I have . . . to be . . . careful. I can be . . . destroyed. I must not . . . allow that to happen. There is much . . . that needs to be done . . . and I am . . . the only Protector. This situation . . . must be set . . . to rights."

"You can be *destroyed*? Not killed?"

"I can be . . . killed."

"But why did you come after me?"

"You . . . ask too many . . . questions."

"Your answer is a lie."

Looking at him, Pasebakhaenniut asked, "Did I not . . . save you?"

"You did," Matt replied. "I have no doubt of that. But you did it for your own reasons."

"I did it . . . because that is . . . what I do."

"Then why do you stay with me now?" Matt countered.

"I don't . . . comprehend."

"You could leave me," Matt said. "Make your own way. You would be faster on your own. I am safe from Creighdor now."

Pasebakhaenniut strode forward, avoiding a rut. His bare feet showed no sign of frostbite. "I would . . . see you home . . . before I go."

"Do you know what my mother taught me was the trouble with lies?" Matt asked.

The mummy didn't reply.

"Once you start a lie, she told me, you have to keep embellishing it to keep it alive. You're with me now for a reason. Something besides merely keeping me safe. Doubtless, Creighdor is already back in London and returned to his schemes. You would be hard-pressed to pick up his trail again."

The mummy ignored him.

"Tell me," Matt demanded after the mummy continued his silence. Matt stopped in the middle of the road. "Tell me now or we'll not proceed another step together. I swear to that. I'll go my own way."

Pasebakhaenniut stopped and glanced around. "There is only one road. There is no other way."

For a moment, Matt felt foolish. He stood his ground stubbornly. "Lucius Creighdor's automaton killed my father before my very eyes," he said in a voice that shook with emotion. "He killed my mother. The man destroyed my family. Don't you understand that? If there is anyone who deserves more to know what this is about, why you are here, then tell me who that is!"

Silently, Pasebakhaenniut looked around at the countryside. "You state your case . . . well, Matt Hunter. But there . . . are things that . . . you must not know. Answers that . . . are not mine . . . to give. Things . . . I must not . . . tell. I am . . . bound . . . by my crafting. A Protector must . . . not interfere . . . with a primitive culture."

"'Primitive'!" Matt exploded. "London is the most advanced city in the world!"

Pasebakhaenniut looked at him. "On this world . . . that is true. That is why . . . the being you call Creighdor . . . has established his . . . beachhead there." He paused. "But . . . it is true. I do want . . . something from you."

The silvery sheen spread throughout Pasebakhaenniut's mouth and throat. A paroxysm shuddered through him. He touched his jaw, shoving it better into place.

"I want to know the location of *Scarlet Moon*," the mummy said, suddenly more clearly than ever. Evidently the surgery automatons within Pasebakhaenniut were still hard at work, because his speech constantly improved as damage was repaired. "I have learned from Creighdor's minions that you know where it is."

"I do." Anticipation whispered through Matt. He hesitated, feeling as though everything balanced on a knife blade. By his admission, if Pasebakhaenniut was willing to torture him and kill him for the information, he had sealed his own doom just as surely as if he had stayed in Dr. Woodard's restraint chair.

"I want you to tell me where that shipwreck is," Pasebakhaenniut said.

"Why?"

"Because what went down on that ship—if it is what Creighdor believes it to be—is mine."

"Yours?"

"Yes."

"Why does Creighdor want it?"

"Because controlling the ship and the weapons on board it will give him even more power than he now possesses. No one will be able to stop him."

"Not even you?"

"He will destroy me with it."

"What is it?"

Pasebakhaenniut shook his head. "As I have said, there are things you may not know and that I may not tell."

"You can't find that shipwreck without me," Matt challenged.

"It would be better if you let me know where it is. Creighdor has already nearly killed you and your friends on several occasions."

"I won't let him get away with what he did to my family."

"Matt Hunter," the mummy said, "I give you my solemn promise that I will see to it Creighdor will pay for his crimes."

"And I give you mine," Matt said fiercely, "that I will be there when Creighdor is made to pay." Without another word, he started forward, leaning into the wind.

Only a moment later, Pasebakhaenniut followed. "You are very stubborn and foolish."

"I," Matt said distinctly, "take great pride in those attributes. They are my father's legacy. I could not hope to be a finer man than he."

Chapter 15

On a cold, blustery afternoon a few days later, riding horses and wearing clothes taken from a group of highwaymen unlucky enough to attack them, Matt and Pasebakhaenniut arrived in London. Bone-weary from the long ride in the winter weather, Matt wanted nothing more than to find a comfortable bed. Only the thought that Creighdor had beaten him back to the city and that his friends might even now be fighting for their lives kept him going.

At a blacksmith's shop he sold the horse for a handful of coins and set out to find one of Gabriel's lads. Matt knew his friends doubtless would be in hiding, even if it was in plain sight so that Creighdor couldn't snare them without someone being the wiser.

Pasebakhaenniut traveled with him, disguised in the heavy winter clothes he wore. The mummy refused to let Matt out of his sight. For his own peace of mind, Matt was reluctant to let the other out of his sight as well. Pasebakhaenniut still had far more answers than he did.

Melting snow made dirty slush piles out in the streets. Coaches sprayed water in all directions as they passed. It was cold enough that Matt's breath puffed out gray in front of him. He noted that Pasebakhaenniut breathed only now and again, about once for every four or five breaths Matt took.

Traveling down from the north side of the city, Matt hailed a coach and they rode to the East End. It was early for Gabriel to be about, but Matt had hopes that one of his lads could seek him out.

Only minutes after arriving in the East End, Matt made contact with one of the boys.

"So you're still alive, then?"

Matt looked up from the bowl of chicken soup he was eating. After leaving word with Gabriel's lad that they would be at the nearby pub, Matt had checked the bill of fare and ordered. The soup was thin and the bread was slightly dried out, but together they seemed to make the perfect meal.

"I am," Matt said.

"God in 'eaven," Gabriel whispered, "I thought I'd never lay me eyes on you again."

"It almost came to that."

Without another word, Gabriel came to him.

Matt stood and met his friend and embraced him tightly for a moment. Seated across the booth, Pasebakhaenniut watched them in silence.

"Who's your friend?" Gabriel asked when they separated. Then he got a better look and took a step back. "That isn't who I think it is, is it?"

"Yes." Matt smiled a little, still having trouble believing it himself.

Gabriel stared at him. "'Ave you taken leave of your senses, then?"

"No."

"Under some kind of spell or somethin'?"

"No," Matt replied. "Sit. Have a cup of tea and I'll explain."

Warily, one hand tucked into a pocket where Matt was sure a pistol was kept, Gabriel sat beside Matt. Returning his attention to the bread and soup, Matt quickly recounted what had happened to him and what Pasebakhaenniut's role in it had been.

Throughout the rest of the afternoon and on into the early evening, Gabriel's lads gathered Matt's friends. Paul and Emma spilled tears at the reunion, clinging to Matt desperately, but Jessie Quinn assured him that she believed him "too ornery to die," as she so colorfully put it, and had never given up hope. Narada Chaudhary was relieved to find Matt still alive and once more free, and even Jaijo seemed pleased at the turn of events.

Later that night, after Matt had attended to a

bath and the change of clothes Paul had brought, they met in one of the hideouts Gabriel had arranged for them. The thief's lads kept watch for Creighdor and gargoyles, but none were seen.

"We tried to find you, Matt," Paul said. "The day you disappeared from jail, I hired private inquiry agents to seek you out. But it was as if you had vanished off the face of the earth."

"I even had my father put some of his people on it," Emma agreed. "But Creighdor has curried too much favor within the queen's court for people to ignore. Everyone assumed you were supposed to quietly fade away. Father's ire has been aroused in this matter. He did not think you should go unpunished for attacking Lord Sanger—"

"'Lord Sanger,'" Matt repeated.

"It is how he is known these days," Emma stated quietly. "He has become quite important to the queen. His gasworks company is expanding throughout the city. Anyway, Father felt you needed proper care in a good asylum with your friends around you rather than being shipped off. In the end, though, he felt certain Lord Sanger had ordered you murdered."

"Not as long as he doesn't have *Scarlet Moon*." Memory of the asylum room and the restraint chair haunted Matt. He didn't look forward to any time spent at sleep and knew he probably wouldn't for a long time to come.

"Well, he's had no time to get it since you escaped from that asylum," Paul said.

From beneath her cowboy hat, Jessie Quinn stared hard at Pasebakhaenniut. "Do we really want to trust him?" Her hands had never been very far from her pistols.

If he took any offense, Pasebakhaenniut didn't show it. The silvery liquid shimmered over his face, constantly struggling to pull his ruined features back into something more pleasing to the eye. Despite the seeming magic the "surgeon automatons" were able to wreak, they never quite succeeded. But at least now skin covered most of his face.

Matt knew that having the mummy with him had unnerved most of his companions. Even after he had told them he was alive now only because of Pasebakhaenniut's help, they remained distrustful.

"It's better that he's with us," Matt said.

"You don't know what you're dealing with," Pasebakhaenniut stated.

Everyone stared at the mummy. During their time with him, the mummy hadn't spoken much. Now they were all astonished by his command of the language.

"Then," Emma said calmly, "why don't you tell us what we're dealing with?"

Pasebakhaenniut shook his head. "As I have explained to Matt Hunter, I can't. I am not permitted."

"Personally, I'd rather tie an anchor to 'im an' drop 'im in the Thames than trust 'im. 'E ain't

never been nothin' but grief for us, 'e ain't."
Gabriel spoke from across the room. He never
got close to the mummy. Part of it was due to his
suspicious nature, but Matt also knew the thief
had a deep and abiding fear of all things super-
natural.

"That course of action wouldn't bode well for
the détente we have managed since Matt's rescue, would it?" Paul asked irritably. "Common
enemies and all that?"

"I'm just sayin' is all. Are you forgettin' 'e can
turn on us any time 'e feels like it."

"Not as long as we can work together,"
Pasebakhaenniut insisted. "Not as long as we
each get what we need. I need what is at the bottom of the ocean, and you need Lucius
Creighdor dead."

"An' who's gonna know when we can't work
together?"

An uncomfortable silence followed.

"I'll tell you who," Gabriel growled, "and
when 'is ownself decides 'e's through with us is
when. Be kind of late by then, don't you think?
We're out on a ship at sea an' all that? Ain't likely
we got many 'oles to 'ide in."

"For the moment," Matt said calmly, "we'll
continue on in this manner, accepting these
alliances at face value." He looked at his companions. "If any of you have objections, I will
understand completely. You're free to leave."

Tension filled the room.

"Lord Brockton," Narada said calmly into the silence that threatened to overwhelm them all, "I don't think any of us clung to hope this long only to desert you at the end."

"It's too late for that, anyway," Jaijo said. "Creighdor has marked us all as enemies. We will live—or die—together."

"An' that just makes me 'appy, it does," Gabriel muttered.

Matt pushed out the breath he hadn't known he was holding. "I know this is uncomfortable, but this how it has to be. With everything Creighdor has aligned against us, we need to move forward."

"Agreed," Paul said. "Since the attack on Creighdor, Hunter Enterprises has suffered several financial setbacks. We are, perhaps, somewhat worse off than when Matt's father was killed. However, I have managed to put back a considerable sum from the profits and we will be solvent for a while yet. We have the wherewithal to continue this war for a time. But only for a time."

"Then we should make the best of it. Do we have the bathysphere and the dive suits?"

"We do," Emma said. "They only became available a few days ago and were brought here. We're still readying everything for the trip."

"What about a ship?"

Paul nodded. "I have recruited Captain Mortimer Stebbins and *Swift Wind* to our mission."

Captain Stebbins had been the ship's commander of *Saucy Lass*, the ketch that had brought in the replacement mummy that Creighdor had used in the Fabulous Harn Museum. In the end, Creighdor had removed Stebbins from his post. Matt had secured the seaman's goodwill and promised him a ship for the information he gave about Creighdor. Stebbins was a good man, well-seasoned to the sea. *Swift Wind* was one of the ships owned by Hunter Enterprises.

"How soon can we leave?" Matt asked.

"In a matter of hours," Paul said. "All that is required is that we transfer the equipment Emma arranged for us. I have kept it separate, hidden and under guard. Not a mean task, I assure you."

"By morning, then," Matt said. "We can't waste any more time."

"There's something else you should know," Gabriel said. "That journalist you sent down to Canterbury?"

"Jeremy Cothern," Matt said.

"Yes. Well, an' he's back."

"When?"

"Three weeks ago."

"Have anyone talked to him?"

"No," Paul said. "We thought it expedient not to draw Creighdor's attention to the man. Gabriel has had his lads keep tabs on him."

"Then you know where Cothern is?"

"Yes," Gabriel answered.

"But we don't know if he's learned anything,"

Paul noted. "It's possible he simply returned to London after learning you'd been . . . detained."

"There's only one way to be sure if Cothern has learned anything of merit." Matt stood. The familiar weight of the Webley pistols was once more in his coat pockets. "We ask him."

Half an hour later, Matt debarked a coach on Fleet Street. Journalists worked in buildings nearly around the clock to gather the latest news and gossip they could use to sell their papers. He was bundled up for winter and wasn't recognizable, so he didn't worry that someone would know him as a fugitive. Matt strode toward Jeremy Cothern's office.

Gabriel and Jessie Quinn went with Matt. As well as Pasebakhaenniut. Paul, Emma, and the Chaudharys made the necessary preparations for their own departure.

During the five weeks of his absence, the papers had been filled with stories of the "mad young Lord Brockton." No doubt the journalists and papers had been inspired by Creighdor's money. They had campaigned solidly against him, quoting physicians who stated that insanity was hereditary. Lady Brockton's murder was once more out in the public eye, and the allusion that Roger Hunter had killed her was stronger than ever.

"Have you seen the baroness?" Jessie asked at his side.

Matt glanced at Jessie.

The girl gave him a coy look. "After you were taken away, the baroness came around. It didn't take long to add two and two. My horse can do that."

Embarrassed, Matt thought quietly for a moment. "Do the others know?"

"You don't have stupid friends, Matt. Emma an' me, we already knew something was goin' on."

"But you said nothing."

"Emma's too polite an' believed it was none of my business."

"You're not polite."

Jessie grinned. "I can be. When I want to."

"Then why didn't you say anything?"

Snorting in feigned disgust, Jessie answered, "Because you're pigheaded an' stupid like a man when it comes to women. It wouldn't have changed your mind if I had, would it?"

"No."

"See? I saved my breath."

Matt continued on for a moment toward his goal, hoping that Cothern was in his office. "Why do you mention it now?"

"Because if you suddenly decided that the baroness should go along on our treasure hunt, you should know it wouldn't work. Trustin' the mummy's hard enough."

"I wasn't going to ask her," Matt said.

That seemed to intrigue Jessie. "Why? Shielding her?"

"I'd shield Emma and you if the two of you would permit it."

"Because we're female?"

"Yes."

Jessie smoothed the brim of her hat with her fingers and smiled. "We won't let you. Back home, I fought coyotes, rustlers, an' Indians. Emma's made of stern stuff too. Real pioneer stock. It's just a shame she's stuck here in this place." She raised an eyebrow. "Course, for the last few months, her life has been mighty interestin'."

All my fault, Matt thought guiltily.

"But I guess maybe you should worry about that little baroness gal," Jessie said.

"The baroness doesn't need protection. I want to keep this as simple as possible. If Csilla journeyed with us, she'd have to bring part of her entourage. Moving that many people would surely attract Creighdor's attention and we'd lose the element of surprise."

"That's good, because I don't much care for the baroness' company. Course, I guess the attraction isn't the same."

Matt decided to let that observation pass without comment. The newspaper office sat just ahead. Questions spun within his mind, and part of him was afraid of the answers he might get.

Chapter 16

The light was on at Jeremy Cothern's office, but the door was locked.

"Let's nip round back," Gabriel suggested. "I'd rather do me breakin' an' enterin' there. Out of sight of any passersby."

They followed the young thief through the alley to the back entrance. Gabriel fitted his lock-picks into the door, silently picked the lock, then opened the door just enough to peek in. He gave a broad, cocky grin at his success.

"Coast is clear," Gabriel whispered.

Unlimbering one of his pistols, Matt opened the door and went into the building. A small storeroom opened into the main room. Cothern's desk was to the left, located in a small area that had once been a broom closet.

The journalist worked with pen and paper, writing speedily, head and shoulders hunched over his work. His brown hair was in disarray, and his suit coat hung on the back of his chair.

Matt paused in the doorway and rapped his pistol barrel against the frame.

Cothern looked up irritably. "I told you not to interrupt me, Hoskins. This piece is due by—" He gulped down the rest of his words and his eyes widened as he saw who stood before him. "Lord Brockton?" he gasped.

"Yes," Matt said calmly. He didn't put the Webley away. Trusting people at this point was a luxury he could ill afford, and trusting the wrong one could get his friends killed.

Recovering slightly, Cothern said, "I thought you were dead."

"Thought? Or hoped?"

Cothern blinked, then recovered. "I did not wish you ill, Lord Brockton."

"The news stories you wrote seem to suggest otherwise." Matt had glanced at several of those on the way over in the coach. Gabriel had rounded them up. None of the stories had favored him, and most of those had concentrated on the murder of Lady Brockton in Canterbury.

"You attacked Lord Sanger," Cothern said.

"I attacked a monster," Matt countered.

"I won't argue that with you." The journalist stared at Matt's pistol. "Are you going to shoot me?"

"Not if I don't have to."

A weak smile twisted Cothern's lips and narrow mustache. "You won't have to, Lord

Brockton. You see, my investigation down in Canterbury was met with partial success."

Interest flared through Matt. After a moment, he put the Webley away. "I'm listening. Come out into the main area so that we may all hear you."

Cothern quit his small office with some reluctance, like a rat leaving its favorite retreat. Shock twisted his features when he saw Pasebakhaenniut.

"This is the mummy everyone has reported seeing?" Cothern whispered.

"Yes," Matt replied.

"This is incredible." Weakly, Cothern sat in the overstuffed chair by the potbelly stove that Matt indicated. "I'd heard stories, but I had no idea that—"

"I don't have much time," Matt said.

Cothern couldn't take his eyes from Pasebakhaenniut. "Some of what I have to tell you may be hard to take, Lord Brockton."

"Not as hard as what I've been through for the last five weeks," Matt assured the journalist.

Cothern shook his head. "There are some things I'm quite certain you don't know. For instance, did you know your mother's condition when she went down to Canterbury with your father?"

"What condition?"

Hesitating, Cothern said, "Lady Brockton was . . . with child. In addition to losing your mother in Canterbury, you also lost a brother or sister. I'm sorry to deliver such bad news."

The words slammed into Matt and took away his breath. *My mother was with child?* The possibility had never occurred to him. His mother had talked about having another child, a brother or a sister for Matt, for years. But it had never come about.

"That fact was left out of all police reports," Cothern said. "But in Canterbury during my investigation I found a midwife who worked for the physician who cared for your mother one night. Lady Brockton took sick and grew concerned about her unborn child. He called on her and gave her medicine that helped her through the sickness. Your mother was very worried."

She would have been, Matt knew. His mother had loved him fiercely and had always been somewhat overprotective.

"I found out about the physician's visit by going through the papers the hotel kept," Cothern said. "I was looking for anything out of the ordinary that might have happened the nights you said your parents were there. After tending to your mother, the physician ate a meal at the hotel and charged it to the account he had at the hotel for being on call for guests. I didn't think anything of the physician's presence for a time, but I followed every lead I could. The only lead left was the midwife."

"My father never said anything of this," Matt

whispered. His brain raced, trying to fit all the pieces together. Nowhere in Roger Hunter's notes was there any mention of his wife's condition.

"I don't think your father knew," Cothern said.

"How could he not?" Matt asked.

"Women," Jessie said succinctly, "have a way of keepin' secrets from menfolk when they want to. If your father didn't know, it was because she didn't want him to know."

"Why would she keep it secret?" The thought hurt Matt.

"Your father was deep into his fight with Creighdor at that point," Jessie said. "Maybe she didn't want to deflect your father's attentions. He was already in jeopardy. An' maybe she just hadn't found the right time to tell him. Tellin' a man he's gonna be a father, even if it's not the first time, is a tricky thing."

"But in Canterbury my mother saw fit to visit a physician," Matt said.

Cothern shook his head. "The physician, Dr. Benjamin Rose, visited your mother at the inn. He didn't know that she was Lady Brockton."

"Didn't know?"

"No." Cothern shook his head. "I burgled Dr. Rose's home and stole his records book. I have it in safekeeping. If you want it, of course it's yours."

"I do." Matt's mouth was dry, and the room

spun. *A brother. A sister.* It all seemed like a night-mare. But during his last memories of his mother, she had asked him if he had his pick would he rather have a little brother or a little sister. "But not now. Now I would have the rest of what you discovered."

"You said the physician didn't know 'e was treatin' Lady Brockton," Gabriel pointed out. "When did 'e up an' figure out the truth?"

"He never did," Cothern said. "At least, I don't believe that he did. It was the midwife who did."

"An' she didn't tell 'er boss?"

"By the time she guessed the truth, after the murder was announced and she saw Lady Brockton's remains, Dr. Rose was also dead."

"'Ow?"

"The midwife found him hanging in his office."

"'E killed 'imself?"

"The midwife didn't think so. Dr. Rose was a stable man. Not given to drink or excesses of any kind. I did follow up on that, with people who had known him, and that was the general con-sensus. Mrs. McHenry thought from the very beginning that some foul play had been done to Dr. Rose. When Lady Brockton's body was later discovered—I do apologize for my blunt man-ner, Lord Brockton."

"Continue," Matt said, willing all the pain and confusion inside him to go away. He could scarcely remain sitting.

"Anyway, after the murder was evident, Mrs.

McHenry felt even more convinced that her employer had been murdered," Cothern said.

"She didn't tell anyone?" Jessie asked.

"With Lady Brockton's murder taking place so soon after Dr. Rose's hanging, Mrs. McHenry was quite convinced that if she told anyone what she knew, her life would be forfeit as well." Cothern paused. "In view of everything, I think she had quite a good grasp of the circumstances."

"An' she chose to take you into 'er confidence, did she?" Gabriel asked.

"Mrs. McHenry has been waiting for years to tell someone that story," Cothern said. "That desire and a pint of brandy, and I heard it all."

"Was there any mention of my mother—of Lady Brockton being seen in Lucius Creighdor's company?" Matt felt like a traitor the instant he asked the question.

Cothern's gaze searched Matt's face. "No, Lord Brockton. None of my inquiries turned up any suggestion of such a meeting taking place."

But that didn't mean it didn't happen, Matt told himself. Creighdor and Scanlon had kidnapped his mother. His father had seen them take her. No one save his father had seen that take place.

He took a deep breath and forced himself to relax. There were still questions he didn't have answers to.

"You had all this information," Jessie said in a harsh voice, "but you didn't come to any of us with it."

"First of all, young lady," Cothern said, "I took employment from Lord Brockton. Not you. Everything I found out would require some release from him before I could tell you."

Jessie glared at him.

Hastily, the journalist added, "I mean no offense, Miss Quinn."

"Keep talkin'," Jessie directed, "while you've still got your teeth. I ain't gettin' any younger."

"After I heard about your . . . *incident* with Lord Sanger," the journalist said, "I returned to London."

Matt stood. "I'll have payment for your time wired to your account in the morning, Mr. Cothern."

Nervous, doubtless wondering how the meeting was truly going to end, Cothern stood as well. "You're most generous, Lord Brockton, in spite of the sadness I have heaped upon you tonight."

"Just remember that I've also brought danger to your doorstep," Matt said. "If Creighdor finds out I've been here, someone may find you dangling from a noose in your office one morning."

Swallowing hard, Cothern nodded. "I'll keep that in mind, milord."

Even after one a.m. in the morning, Dr. Harrison Fletcher opened his own door. He held a small candle lantern in an arthritic hand and peered up at Matt.

"Is it an emergency?" Dr. Fletcher asked. He fumbled in his nightshirt pocket for his glasses and put them on, knocking his pointed nightcap askew.

"It is for me, Dr. Fletcher," Matt answered. He felt empty and hollow from everything he had learned from Cothern. But before he departed London, he had to verify the story. There was only one person left alive who might be able to do that.

"What is the matter?" The physician was in his early seventies but was still quick of mind and able of body. He raised the candle and gazed at Matt.

"Do you know me, sir?" Matt was polite and tried to keep his voice calm. He wasn't sure if he had succeeded.

"Of course I do," Dr. Fletcher snapped. "You're Matthew Hunter. Lord Brockton these days, I suppose."

"Yes, sir." Matt hesitated. Jessie, Gabriel, and Pasebakhaenniut sat in the coach out in the street. The horses' breaths made gray plumes from the cold.

"You're supposed to be in prison or some such, aren't you?" Dr. Fletcher asked. "For attacking Lucius Creighdor?"

"An asylum, actually," Matt said. "Yes sir, I am. I . . . escaped."

"Escaped, you say? Well, are you in your right

mind now?"

"I am, sir. Thank you for your concern."

Dr. Fletcher waved the acknowledgment away. "I didn't ask out of concern for you. I asked out of concern for me. If I have a madman at my door, I should think I have the right to know."

"Yes, sir."

"Do you want to come in?"

"I'm afraid there isn't time. I'm in a bit of a hurry."

Poking his head out the door, Dr. Fletcher peered up and down the street. "There's no sign of the police."

"No, sir," Matt said. "I don't think they know yet. It was a good escape."

"Well then, bully for you."

"Sir?"

"I've never liked that man Creighdor. I've always believed him to be as crooked and conniving as Lord Broc—as your father stated he was." Dr. Fletcher harrumphed.

"Creighdor is," Matt replied. "But his guilt is hard to prove, I'm afraid."

"Well then, what do you plan to do?"

Matt smiled. "Prove that Creighdor's just as corrupt as my father said he was."

Dr. Fletcher nodded and clapped Matt on the shoulder. "The day I delivered you, I told your father that you were going to be a man like him. I could feel it in your bones. You came into this world a fighter. I suspect you'll go out the same way." He ran his gaze over Matt. "What do you need from an old, broken-down doctor who's too stubborn to completely retire?"

"I need to know about my mother, Dr. Fletcher."

"Poor Angeline," the physician whispered. Sadness touched his rheumy eyes. "Such a terrible thing, God rest her soul."

Be strong, Matt told himself. *Now is not the time for weakness.* He forced himself to speak. "I was only recently told that my mother at the time of her death . . . was with child, Dr. Fletcher."

Taken aback, the old physician stared at Matt. "That's a hard thing you've come asking after."

"I know that. But I need to know if it was true." *You did not immediately deny it, did you?*

"Why?"

Matt took a deep breath. "It concerns Lucius Creighdor."

"How?"

"I don't yet know, sir. You'll have to take my word that I have a valid reason for asking."

Sighing, the old physician nodded. "Lady Brockton was with child at the time of her death, son. I never told anyone because it was no one's business except hers. And her husband's, eventually, I suppose."

"Did my father ever know?"

"When we talked after your mother's demise, your father never mentioned it. I assumed Lady

Brockton had never gotten round to it. Women have their own time and place for letting a man know things like that."

"Yes, sir."

"Afterward . . ." Dr. Fletcher shrugged. "Well, I never had the heart to tell your father. He, as well as Lady Brockton, was my friend. After all that he had lost, after all that he had suffered, he didn't need to know about one more thing that would have hurt him." The physician looked at Matt. "Nor do you, my boy."

Matt took a deep breath and made himself go on. "Did Creighdor know? About my mother?"

Pain twisted Dr. Fletcher's face. His hand shook so much that he almost dropped the candle. Matt took it from him and held it, but found his own hand wasn't steady either.

Your mother, in a sense, birthed both of us. Creighdor's words, spoken at the asylum, haunted Matt now. Kesel's voice bounced around inside his brain as well. *Creighdor . . . somehow he discovered the secret of immortality. He needed the salvaged flesh that we grew so specially.*

"Doctor," Matt said in a hoarse voice, "did Lucius Creighdor know about my mother's condition?"

For a moment, Dr. Fletcher didn't answer. His voice broke when he finally responded. "Yes. I learned from your mother later that Creighdor had sent your mother flowers—roses, I believe—congratulating her on the coming birth. She asked me about it later, of course."

A great weight seemed to lift from Matt's shoulders. The note had been in his mother's handwriting, but Dr. Woodward had presented it out of context. His mother had simply written Creighdor out of politeness, with no nefarious doings at all connected to it. "Do you know how Creighdor found out?"

"I was terribly embarrassed," the old physician said. "As you know, medical ills are a private matter, and I pride myself on being close-mouthed about these things. As it turns out, I had a young doctor working for me. A young man named James Dorrance. He was a friend of Creighdor's and he told me he had happened to mention your mother's delicate condition before he thought to stop himself."

Matt recognized the name immediately. Dr. James Dorrance had been the physician Creighdor had used to breed the brain parasites and infect patients like Nigel Kirkland.

"A few months ago," Dr. Fletcher continued, "I read in the paper that James Dorrance had mysteriously disappeared. You'll get no apology from him unless he shows up again."

Matt knew what had happened to Dorrance. The doctor had died a hideous death in a vat of the brain parasites. Matt had caused the physician's demise.

"Thank you for your time, Doctor." Matt turned to walk away. Emotions whirled within him, creating a confusion that drained him. He concentrated on his anger and held to it fiercely. Anger seemed to give him direction and purpose.

"Lord Brockton," Dr. Fletcher called.

Matt looked at the small, gnarled man who had delivered him. "Yes, sir."

"Be careful, lad," Dr. Fletcher said. "I know that most people in this city believe your father took his own life."

"I don't," Matt said.

"Nor do I." Dr. Fletcher grimaced and spoke softly. "You've a powerful enemy waiting out there, Lord Brockton."

"I know," Matt said. "That's part of my father's legacy. I mean to honor it."

Chapter 17

Matt woke with the sound of waves in his ears and the smell of the salty sea in the air. A strong winter chill pervaded the ship's cabin. He moved cautiously, swaying in the hammock, then got up.

The deck rolled beneath his feet. He'd been away from ships for too long. He didn't have his sea legs, but he knew from experience they would come back quickly. He climbed the ladder and went up on deck.

For a moment, standing on deck with the sails bloomed full above him and the wind blowing through his hair, Matt felt at peace in the world, even in the biting cold. But the moment didn't last. Memory of Lucius Creighdor and what he and his friends—and Pasebakhaenniut—had come to do interrupted that feeling.

Swift Wind hurtled across the North Sea. The ship was a fast three-master, built cunningly to drive through the waves. Captain Stebbins was an old hand at getting the most out of his vessels.

Late afternoon sunlight turned the western sky red and gold. They were far enough out from the coast that England couldn't be seen anymore. Gray and black terns coasted on the breeze overhead. Around the ship, whitecaps churned across the gray-green sea on tall waves that slapped against the hull.

Covered by heavy canvas, the bathysphere was a round shape nearly twice the height of a man. Ropes crisscrossed the diving device, lashing it to the deck.

"Matt."

Emma stood on the rear deck. She wore a long jacket to protect her against the cold.

Matt went up the stairwell and joined her. Narada and Paul were with Pasebakhaenniut and Captain Stebbins at the small desk by the ship's wheel, poring over the map Cyrus Stewart had guided them to. The crew still stared at the mummy, but none of them said anything. Paul had claimed that for the wages they were paying them, the sailors should have crewed to the edge of the world without complaint.

"How do you feel?" Emma asked.

"Tired," Matt said. "Restless." He shook his head. "I don't know."

"You went through a lot last night," she told him.

After he'd arrived at the ship, Matt had

helped ready the vessel for the journey. He'd also told the others who hadn't gone with him to Cothern's office what he had found out.

"I shouldn't have slept so long," Matt said, feeling guilty.

"Nonsense," Emma protested. "You needed to rest. There's nothing any of us can do aboard this ship. We're all in Captain Stebbins's capable hands during this leg of the voyage."

Matt stared at the canvas-covered shape. "And when we reach the site?"

"Then we're in Professor Robeson's capable hands."

Professor Pierre Robeson was the ocean specialist who was Emma's friend. Matt vaguely remembered meeting him last night while boarding *Swift Wind*. In his early thirties, the professor was lean and energetic, with a neatly trimmed reddish beard, glasses, and unruly blond hair.

"Until that time, you're in my hands, Lord Brockton." Emma smiled at him. "First, you'll eat. Then I'm going to do something about that beard and that wild mane you've grown. There's no reason for you to look uncivilized."

During the next three days, *Swift Wind* remained under full sail. Freshly shaved and shorn, Matt made himself as useful as he could around the ship—mending, repairing, and painting—but the captain and his crew worked sharply together and there was little to do. Inactivity—when it felt like he hovered on the brink of doom—frustrated him. He lived for physical labor and vigorously applied himself to it.

Lookouts maintained vigilance over the sea. No other ships they infrequently passed took undue interest in them. *Swift Wind* traveled unimpeded.

Emma taught Matt how to use the dive suits and acquainted him with the inside of the bathysphere. Matt found the sea-diving vessel too cramped for his liking and felt claustrophobic. He knew those feelings would only be amplified when he was submerged in it. Despite his anxiousness to reach the shipwreck site, he didn't look forward to spending time in the bathysphere.

When he wasn't working or learning about the dive equipment, Matt planned. He still didn't know what Creighdor's schemes were.

"I think Creighdor plans on doing something with the renovations he's done to the gas lines under the city," Paul said on the evening of the third day.

Matt sat at one of the tables in the ship's galley. A plateful of chops and potatoes and gravy held his attention. "What makes you say that?"

On the other side of the table, Paul opened the valise he carried and spread out maps. "I took the liberty of quietly procuring these blueprints from the engineering agencies that issued licenses on the new systems. I figured that anything

Creighdor was doing, especially something that won him a title from the queen, was well-worth our efforts to research. I believe I was correct."

Matt surveyed the blueprints. "You bribed government officials?"

"They weren't exactly government officials," Paul said with a little discomfort.

Despite the mood that filled him, Matt couldn't help but smile a little. Bribing government officials wasn't something the Paul Chadwick-Standish he knew would do. But thinking what had driven his friend to that length was sobering.

"That's splitting hairs, I know," Paul admitted.

"I'm not going to fault you, Paul. Rather, I should compliment you on your resourcefulness."

"Well," Paul said, "you should be commended as well, then."

"Me?" Matt lifted an eyebrow.

"I did bribe them with your money. A shameful excess, actually."

Matt laughed aloud, startling them both. Paul joined in, and for a moment they could not stop. It felt good to simply let go for a short time, and Matt knew they both needed the release.

Finally, Paul said, "What I'd like to draw your attention to is this." He pointed to the blueprints. "London gasworks companies have always maintained exclusivity and territorial privilege. None of them have allowed others to tie into their lines. The general consensus is that if one system fails, the other lines will remain intact. Lucius Creighdor's additions have changed all that."

"How?"

"He has created a central exchange network that links all of the other companies' lines," Paul said. "It allows the other lines to remain separate, but he can access them."

Matt was puzzled. Distracted by the discoveries he hoped to make at the shipwreck site, he had trouble focusing. "To what purpose?"

"On the surface, his systems are there to increase gas pressure in areas when some companies fail to reach the necessary minimums."

"But that makes sense." While living in London, Matt had known days when the gas pressure wasn't the best. "Some families have frozen to death during cold winters when enough gas couldn't be supplied." Many homes and businesses had converted over to gas systems so they wouldn't have to truck in or keep wood supplies on hand.

"Of course it makes sense," Paul argued. "That's why the queen gave Creighdor a title for his efforts. But I also know that Creighdor has always looked toward the profit-and-loss situations of his investments. This latest venture is surely going to lose money for him."

"So the reason for building the new lines isn't financial?"

Paul nodded. "That is my assumption."

"Then why build it?"

"That is the question, isn't it?"

On the morning of the next day, *Swift Wind* reached the area where *Scarlet Moon* had sunk. The crew furled the sails and they sat at anchor under a dark sky filled with the threat of impending storm. Choppy waves slammed against the ship without rest.

"You're sure this is the place?" Matt asked.

Narada traced his finger along Cyrus Stewart's map where it lay protected under glass at the navigator's station. "This is it, Lord Brockton. We've found the given landmarks." He handed Matt a spyglass.

Turning the glass toward the distant coastline, Matt sought out the landmarks. The reef that had ripped *Scarlet Moon*'s bottom out all those years ago showed up as gnarled veins to the southeast.

What was left of *Scarlet Moon* lay somewhere on the ocean bottom. It was still a considerable amount of space to search.

Paul glanced out over the water. "The shipwreck has to be here."

"Unless the current's swept it out to sea," Gabriel said. He hadn't been happy the last few days. As they had all found out, sailing didn't agree with him. He'd spent most of the time with seasickness.

"Let's hope it hasn't," Matt said.

Emma, dressed in man's clothing, stood at *Swift Wind*'s starboard railing and drew up a knotted cord. "The bottom's seventy-two feet below."

"The bathysphere is safe to that depth?" Matt asked.

"Yes."

Matt looked at the canvas-covered vessel sitting amidships on *Swift Wind*. "Then let's be about it while we still have the light."

Pasebakhaenniut crossed to the railing and peered down into the ocean. "You're sure this is the place, Matt Hunter?"

"If the map is accurate," Matt answered, "then yes."

Without another word, Pasebakhaenniut leaped into the water and disappeared.

"I guess," Gabriel said in a soft voice, "maybe 'e forgot 'is suit. Or maybe 'e can 'old 'is breath a really long time."

"I'm not sure he breathes," Matt said. Then he went to get suited up.

"Can you breathe all right?"

Even though Paul was standing in front of him and shouting, Matt barely heard his friend. The massive dive helmet muted all noise—except for the rapid popping of the air compressor that would keep him alive on the ocean floor. The dive suit felt clunky and heavy, especially with the weighted shoes.

"I can breathe," Matt said. Out of habit he tried to nod but he only succeeded in bumping his head inside the dive helmet. The air pumped into the helmet tasted strangely metallic, but he was grateful for it.

Paul looked worried as he stepped back. Despite Emma's enthusiasm and experience with the equipment, Paul didn't care for it. "Might be better to wait until after this storm blows over."

To the east, the sky swirled with black clouds and partially hidden lightning.

"An' that might be the storm that finally does for what's left of that ship," Gabriel said. Like Paul and Jaijo, Gabriel was staying aboard *Swift Wind* to man the air lines while Matt, Jessie, Emma, and Professor Robeson searched the ocean floor for the shipwreck. Narada and one of Professor Robeson's assistants were going down in the bathysphere.

"Time is against us," Matt said. "We have to go now and hope for the best." Taking care not to tangle the all-important air lines, he walked to *Swift Wind's* port side, opened the gate, and stepped through.

Weighed down by the suit, Matt carefully climbed down the fishing net the sailors had attached to the ship's side to serve as a ladder. The ocean was nearly freezing as it climbed up his body. Only the additional layers of clothing under the suit kept him warm.

At the bottom of the net, Matt paused to check the rope that Gabriel laid out. The rope would serve to be his guide back to the ship as well as a way of bringing him back in case he got into trouble.

Matt gave Gabriel a final thumbs-up. Then he let go the net and fell through the ocean depths. He dropped slowly, arms instinctively thrown out to catch himself. Unfortunately, there was nothing to catch and the heavy iron boots dragged him relentlessly to the ocean bottom.

Being under that much water, Matt discovered, felt a lot like he would imagine it would feel to be buried alive. As he dropped, he felt the water pressure close in on him as Emma had explained it would. Also, the water darkened around him as the light failed to penetrate the depths. By the time he reached the bottom, seventy-two feet down, he knew he would only be able to see a few feet in any direction.

At the bottom of the long drop, Matt landed on his feet. A startled hermit crab darted away, stirring up sand as it scuttled. Schools of fish hung in the water.

For a moment, Matt stood transfixed. Even though Emma had told him of her experiences while diving, of the thrill and wonder of it all, he still wasn't prepared for the sheer amazement that struck him.

Minutes passed as he peered around in wonder. Then the rope tied round his waist pulled at him. It was Gabriel, asking if he was all right.

Matt pulled once on the rope, letting Gabriel know he was fine. Three quick jerks at either end would signal it was time to go.

Moving slowly, impeded by the ocean, Matt began walking. Emma and Professor Robeson had marked out a grid while planning aboardship, but had admitted that once below, none of them would be able to walk the pattern exactly. The waterproof compass on his wrist at least gave Matt the right idea of which direction to go.

He went north, taking deeper breaths than he was accustomed to. The air in his lungs felt turgid, and he had to force each breath.

The ocean floor was a pristine wasteland. Except for occasional rock, plants, and some kind of strange coral formations that Matt was willing to bet Emma would know the name of, the sea bottom was covered by sand. Every step Matt took, impossibly slow and ponderous, stirred up sand. The cold pressed in at him. He tried desperately not to think that more than seventy feet of water separated him from the surface.

Despite the cold ocean, Matt soon found his clothing was soaked from his exertions. A malaise filled him as he stayed on his course. Thoughts of his parents and unborn sibling collided again and again inside his head.

Two short jerks on the rope dragged his attention back to the present. Two jerks meant he'd reached the end of his first route.

He turned to his left, looked as far as he could, and saw nothing. Then he checked the compass and turned south, walking back in the same area. By moving over slightly, to the degree his vision would penetrate the gloom, each of the dive members could gradually cover the area assigned to them.

This time he walked under the bathysphere that Narada and the assistant manned. Specially protected lights, powered by a generator aboard *Swift Wind*, shined into the depths. A boom arm moved the bathysphere through the ocean, farther and farther down.

At the bathysphere, Matt turned around and walked back. Two circuits later, on the outward leg of his search pattern, something slapped him on the helmet. Turning, he found himself face-to-face with a dead man.

Chapter 18

Shoving the dead man away, Matt backpedaled in the ocean and shouted. His heart lurched inside his chest. The sand beneath the heavy iron boots slipped and he fell—slowly—to the ocean floor. On his back, with the limited vision of the dive helmet, he lost sight of the dead man but felt certain the attack would come at any moment. He lifted his gloved hands before him.

Nothing happened.

Calming himself, Matt pushed himself back to his feet. The task was easier than he'd thought it would be. Once more erect, he stared in the direction he'd seen the dead man, thinking maybe he'd just imagined it. Emma had mentioned that some divers had nightmares while underwater, an indication it was time for that diver to resurface.

But the dead man was right where he'd seen him.

The corpse was little more than bones wrapped in ragged clothing. One of its feet was tangled in a length of rotted net mired by a ship's anchor. The body hung, looking animated as it slowly twisted and turned.

Excitement filled Matt. He tried to keep his feelings in perspective. *Finding a dead man down here doesn't mean you've found* Scarlet Moon, he told himself. *The seas are full of dead sailors.*

He walked over to the skeleton and examined it. Tiny fish darted in and out of the empty eye hollows and open jaws.

Leaving the body drifting on the net, Matt went forward through the murky water. A few feet farther on, he came across debris from a shipwreck. *Scarlet Moon* had hit the hidden reef, driven by a storm that night. After she'd ripped her bottom out, she hadn't gone down whole; she'd gone down in pieces. This must be it.

Matt paused and yanked on the tether twice. The signal went to Gabriel, letting him know that Matt had located the wreck.

The rope pulled back twice. Gabriel would call out the information to the other crew manning the three other divers. All would converge on Matt's location.

Matt topped a rise before he knew it, then saw a green light glowing in the darkness ahead. He stopped and drew the long-bladed fighting knife taped to his leg. Eighteen inches of hammered metal provided a decent weapon underwater. He continued on.

Slowly, the hulk of the shipwreck came into view. The green light flicked back and forth. Then Matt saw Pasebakhaenniut swimming toward the ship. Evidently the mummy had found the shipwreck at nearly the same time while walking his own grid.

If it's the right shipwreck, Matt thought as he walked down into the depression that shielded the sunken ship.

Scarlet Moon lay partially on her side with her prow buried in the side of a rolling hill. Pasebakhaenniut swam effortlessly. No air bubbles followed in his wake. Matt didn't know if Pasebakhaenniut had been underwater the whole time or if he had occasionally gone up for air. But the freezing water didn't seem to bother him.

At the ship, Matt crawled cautiously onto it. He moved slowly and almost effortlessly underwater, but he took care not to get his air line or tether fouled. Either one of those could cause fatal problems.

Pasebakhaenniut kneeled amidship, then dropped through the cargo hold.

Abandoning his perch, Matt went forward across the tilted deck to the captain's quarters. The door was locked tight. He used the fighting knife to slip the bolt.

If this device was something valuable, he realized, *it wouldn't have been kept with the common cargo.* The most obvious place to search was the captain's quarters.

When he opened the door, a school of fish exploded out at him. Several of them struck the dive helmet with dull thunks. Then they were gone.

As he surveyed the cabin's darkened interior, Matt wished he had an underwater lantern of some kind. He set to work, going through the captain's chest, the desk built into the wall, and the cabinets built over the window set into the stern. At last he found the device in a craftily designed hiding place under the bed.

Excitement flared through Matt as he studied the object. It was obviously manmade, but unlike anything he'd ever seen before. All the past months of searching for answers as to why his mother had been so foully murdered, of what Creighdor was trying to keep hidden by killing his father, welled up inside him till the emotion was almost overpowering.

Matt stood frozen for a moment, afraid to touch it in case it disappeared. *Please,* he thought, *please let this be real.* He wished for that so badly, it almost made him sick.

With a shaking hand he reached for the treasure. His gloved fingers slid over it. He missed the feeling of touch. Trapped inside the protective dive suit, he couldn't feel the box. But it was *real.*

It was wrapped in oilskin, protecting it from water. Unfortunately, during the wreck the oilskin had come loose and let the ocean in. Knowing he couldn't hurt his find any more, he unwrapped it.

The device was a metal rectangle two feet long by one foot wide by six inches thick. Unbelievably, it showed no signs of rust or pitting. As far as Matt knew, the only metal that didn't rust in salt water was gold. Even silver coins were eaten away by the corrosive nature of the sea. But this was not gold.

Turning the device to better catch the light, Matt made out a design of a strange ship in bas-relief on the top. It was not like any ship Matt had ever seen. There were no open decks or sails. Rather, the vessel was closed like one of the armored ships, *Monitor* and *Merrimac*, the Americans had built during their War Between the States.

But this ship was different. Instead of looking ungainly, this vessel resembled a hawk or a bird of prey.

Sensing someone watching him, he looked up.

Pasebakhaenniut stood in the doorway, face devoid of emotion. The lack of color in the sea, rendering everything in lights and darks, made him look more corpselike than ever.

For a moment, Matt waited for the mummy to attack. He clutched the knife in his hand and made himself remember that Pasebakhaenniut had come for him in the asylum. *To show him this place, though, not out of friendship.*

Pasebakhaenniut reached for the rectangle and gestured.

Reluctantly, Matt handed the device over. *For all I know, he can swim to London from here. Or anywhere else he wants to go.* If Pasebakhaenniut decided to take off, Matt knew he would never be able to stop him.

Reverently, the mummy knelt and pressed his hand against the top of the rectangle. Green light pulsed through his flesh, gleaming along the metal rods that lay along his fingers and the back of his hand.

The rectangle opened, splitting down the middle and folding up like a bench seat. Incredibly, a three-dimensional image formed a few inches above the surface. Gazing at it, Matt was instantly reminded of the images that had poured from the mummy's eyes aboard *Saucy Lass.*

Pasebakhaenniut ran his fingers along the device. Symbols formed on the ship's image in glowing red and purple. Apparently he was satisfied with what he found, because he closed the rectangle and tucked it under one arm. A brief search of the rest of the cabin turned up another case like the first one, only a little bigger and more square in shape, but nothing further. The mummy motioned Matt to follow him, then left the captain's quarters.

Outside, Matt met Emma, Jessie, and Professor Robeson crawling across the wreckage. They had surfaced and then followed Matt's tether back down below.

Even out in the open now, Matt could barely see across the few feet that separated him from the others. They were losing the light, either to the end of day or to the storm.

Pasebakhaenniut pointed up, then took hold of Matt's tether and started climbing. Matt followed the mummy, crawling tiredly through the depths. The others trailed after them, each climbing their own tether. They passed the bathysphere on the way up, but the winch aboard *Swift Wind* was hauling up the metal ball as well.

Long minutes later, Matt surfaced and found that the storm had closed in on *Swift Wind*. Jagged lightning scored the sky, and rain drummed the ocean surface. Thunder boomed, muted somewhat as it filtered through the dive helmet. Fog slid in clouds across the ocean.

Grabbing hold of the net at the ship's side, Matt opened his faceplate and looked for Pasebakhaenniut. When he saw the mummy bobbing in the water beside him, he asked, "Is that it, then? Is that what we came for?"

"Yes," Pasebakhaenniut replied.

"What is it?"

"I am sorry, Matt Hunter, but I cannot tell you."

Anger hammered Matt then. "I will not settle

for that answer. Not anymore. I lost my family to Creighdor and whatever it is that's been hidden for all these years. You owe me that, Pasebakhaenniut. If it weren't for me, if it weren't for my father's sacrifices, you would not have that device now. I don't know what you are or where you come from, but if you have any sense of honor, you know my friends and I are owed those answers."

Pasebakhaenniut regarded him in silence for a long time, bobbing gently on the water. Finally, he said, "I will try. Once we are onboard the ship."

Chapter 19

Hours later, Matt and his companions met with Pasebakhaenniut in the captain's cramped quarters. They sat huddled in blankets, trying to reclaim the warmth the cold water and the storm had leeched from them. Emma had prepared chowder and strong tea, and there was plenty of it.

Pasebakhaenniut reflected, obviously gathering his thoughts. Then he brought out the rectangle Matt had recovered from *Scarlet Moon*, opened it, and made the three-dimensional shape of the strange ship appear again.

Emma poked her finger at the image hesitantly. The image bent, then re-formed when she removed her finger. "Amazing," she whispered.

"This is the ship that brought me here," Pasebakhaenniut announced.

"To Egypt?" Gabriel asked.

"No," Pasebakhaenniut answered. "To this world."

"You're sayin' you're from another world?" Gabriel grinned like he was in on the joke.

"I am."

"You're serious?" Gabriel's voice sounded strained.

"I would not tell you this," Pasebakhaenniut declared, "if Matt Hunter had not forced me to."

No one said anything for a time, then Emma asked, "What world are you from? Mars? Venus?" She was obviously struggling to believe what the mummy said. "Those are the ones closest to us, though no one believes anyone really lives on those planets."

"From neither of those," Pasebakhaenniut said. "I don't come from any of the nine planets in your solar system."

"There aren't nine planets," Emma objected. "There are only eight."

Pasebakhaenniut paused, then nodded. "As you say. There is one body that may or may not be called a planet by your people's criteria."

Emma looked like she wanted to object again.

Knowing how important science was to her, Matt cut in before she could say anything. "Where do you come from?"

What Pasebakhaenniut said was unpronounceable, Matt was sure, by anyone human.

"Is that the same world as Creighdor is from?" Matt asked.

"No. Creighdor and his people come from another world in a different star system. The beings who created me were peaceful. Creighdor's kind are all bloodthirsty barbarians who live to kill and conquer."

"You landed here during the time of the Egyptians," Narada said.

"Exactly."

"Why?"

Pasebakhaenniut gazed at the image on the device before him. "It was not a choice. Any of us being here, it wasn't a choice. On my world, I am a Protector."

"What is that?" Paul asked.

"An artificial being would be the closest description in your language, I suppose. Your understanding of science is . . . primitive at best. Suffice to say, I was built through specialized engineering, not born of flesh and blood."

"Like one of Creighdor's gargoyles?" Gabriel asked.

"No. Those are limited . . . automatons. They don't truly think for themselves. At best, they possess an animal's intelligence and instincts. I have been constructed to be an independent intelligence. I can formulate plans and opinions, and make judgments. Those qualities are important in a Protector. What I do is much like the service your bobbies provide."

"Or a Texas Ranger," Jessie said. "Sort of a . . . space ranger."

"I don't know anything about Texas Rangers," Pasebakhaenniut said.

"What do you protect?" Matt asked.

"My people. Back on my world, there is . . . there was a war going on. A war that involved several planets and several solar systems. We have star-drive capabilities that allow us to . . . jump through . . . holes in space. It was during one of those jumps that the prison ship I was piloting was ambushed and nearly destroyed."

"A prison ship?" Matt repeated. "Was Creighdor on that ship?"

"The being you know as 'Creighdor' was a murderer, a thief, and a spy long before we crashed onto your planet. Seizing him was an important part of our war efforts."

"How did you get to Egypt?" Narada asked.

"The ship crashed in the immense desert near there. Many of my prisoners were killed. I was nearly destroyed. If it hadn't been for the 'surgeon automatons' designed within my body, I would have been. The escapees thought I had perished. They did not know the extent of my abilities. My body took time to reconstruct, but I followed the trail of the escapees. By that time they had enmeshed themselves in the Egyptian culture. I had to ferret them out."

"But you can't be a machine," Emma protested. "I opened up your chest myself. I saw where you once had a heart, lungs, and the rest of your organs."

"I am still an artificial construct, Miss Sharpe," Pasebakhaenniut insisted. "The body is amazing. Flawless design. When my creators sought to make artificial people, they modeled them on the their bodies. I've just been . . . enhanced from the original concept."

"But Creighdor is human?" Jessie asked.

"As you understand the term, yes. He is like you. He was born of a mother and father, not brought to life in a laboratory."

"But how has Creighdor managed to live so long?" Paul asked.

"One of the reasons his race has been abhorred everywhere is due to their capacity to cannibalize others for their own needs. They are ultimate survivors, able to take organs and tissues from others and utilize them to rejuvenate their own bodies. If their old body is destroyed, they can transplant their brains, and sometimes only their consciousness if the original brain is damaged, into other bodies that have been built for them."

"That's what Creighdor has been doing here," Matt whispered. Horror at what had probably been done to his mother and his unborn sibling chilled him.

"Yes. Creighdor was trained on his world to manage that process. Only a select few are given the knowledge and training he had. He first started that practice among the Egyptians, taking slaves for his needs," Pasebakhaenniut said.

"Gradually, Creighdor made himself more like you, but that weakened him. When one of the prisoners from the transport ship died, Creighdor experimented on that body by taking organs out and putting organs back in. Eventually, he made the process he'd learned on his home world work here as well. But he continued working, searching for a way to make blending your species with his own more . . . amenable. He worked on the process for years. Judging from his efforts with Dr. Kesel, he was still working on them."

"That was what Dr. Kesel was talking about when Matt confronted him," Emma said. "Creighdor had him work on those experiments."

"Yes," Pasebakhaenniut said.

"Why didn't you stop Creighdor?" Jessie asked.

"I tried, but Creighdor's escaped from me on several occasions. I am not infallible, simply hard to kill. Finally, while we were in Egypt, Creighdor caught me in a trap and killed me. At least, as close to being dead as I've ever experienced. Normally, the surgeon automatons that are part of me would have begun repair. But Creighdor hollowed me out, scavenged my organs, and depleted the power source. My automatons were unable to perform their function. The mummification treatment further inhibited my regenerative ability. The surgeon automatons were rendered inert, but not destroyed as Creighdor believed."

"Until we ran electricity through your body," Emma said.

Pasebakhaenniut nodded. "While he has been here, Creighdor has used his understanding of science to further his own interests. He employs the gargoyles as sentinels and the mind parasites to control others."

"Creighdor invented the mind parasites?" Matt asked.

"No. Those were mine. As a Protector, I used them as restraints, a way of keeping a prisoner sedate and pliable during a shipboard journey. I was the only Protector onboard for the prisoner transportation."

"They were like 'andcuffs then," Gabriel said.

"Yes. During the crash in the desert, several of the mind parasites—as you call them—were destroyed within their hosts. After he killed me, Creighdor obviously took some of them with him and only lately has figured out a way to replicate them for his own uses."

Matt pointed to the device that displayed the ship image. "What is that?"

"A device that allows me to control and communicate with my ship. It's . . . central cortex. A 'brain,' I suppose you would call it. I took it out after the crash."

"If your ship is damaged," Paul said, "why would you need it?"

"I believe my ship can be repaired," Pasebakhaenniut said. "It will take time. Perhaps more time than I realize while I wait for your technology to grow. But I don't age. I won't die from most causes. I have time to wait. But I can't operate the ship without this unit. In the meantime, I intend to track down Creighdor and the other prisoners that I lost when my ship crashed thousands of years ago."

"How many?" Matt asked quietly. "How many prisoners did you have on that ship?"

"Three hundred seventeen," Pasebakhaenniut answered. "Two hundred forty-three are still in stasis aboard the ship where it's buried in the desert."

"That leaves seventy-four unaccounted for," Paul stated.

"Yes, but of the seventy-four that escaped, I have killed forty-nine. Most of those met their fate back in Egypt."

"That leaves twenty-five."

"Twenty-five," Pasebakhaenniut said, "is a much better number than three hundred seventeen."

"What will you do with them when you find them?" Matt asked.

"Take them back into custody, or kill them."

"I didn't think they could be killed," Paul said.

"They can be killed," Matt said. "I've seen him do it." He remembered how

Pasebakhaenniut had yanked the man Dwight's head off and how the body had faded from sight.

"You can kill them," Pasebakhaenniut agreed. "If you remove their heads with no bodies or devices to copy their consciousness into, they discorporate. That feature is programmed into them at birth so that their corpses can't fall into the hands of their enemies to be studied. They're very protective of the process Creighdor uses to keep himself alive."

"You're only going to get Creighdor one way," Matt promised. "After everything he's done to my family, he's going to die. I will be his judgment."

Later, after the meeting had broken up, Matt couldn't sleep. *Swift Wind* sailed across the ocean, running under full sail as she made her way back to London. He stood at the rail and tried to organize his thoughts. His emotions, feelings of loss and anger and fear, kept getting in the way.

Emma joined him after a few minutes, bringing him a steaming cup of tea. "It's fresh," she said.

Matt took the cup and relished the heat it offered. He held it in both hands. "Thank you."

Silence stretched out long and lean between them for a while.

Finally Emma got around to what was on her mind as he knew she would. "Do you believe him?" she asked.

Matt knew she was talking about Pasebakhaenniut. "Yes."

"Really now, Matt. People from other planets?"

"Do you have another answer?"

"No."

"Then we'll go with that one," Matt said.

"There's still no guarantee Pasebakhaenniut won't betray us."

"No," Matt agreed. "But I trust him. After everything we've been through, I might even like him."

"He looks like a monstrosity."

Matt smiled. "I know. But he fights like a regiment. With what we're facing, I can only hope that Pasebakhaenniut remains on our side. I would hate to have him as an enemy."

Chapter 20

Days later, Matt and his friends returned to London in the dead of night, wary of traps Creighdor might have set.

Pasebakhaenniut was dressed in a heavy coat that reached to his boots. A hood shadowed his face. He wouldn't be able to walk around in open daylight, but even Jessie—the most outspoken critic of the group—deemed the mummy passable in the night.

They took coaches to a flat in the East End that Gabriel had arranged.

"I believe Paul's assessment of Creighdor's new gasworks is correct," Narada said as they contemplated the blueprints on the table. "It promises some kind of threat."

"A threat?" Gabriel repeated. "What kind of threat? Do you think Creighdor will shut down the gas an' let everybody die from the cold?"

"No," Narada said. "Of course not. Even if Creighdor did that, not everyone would die."

"Upon seeing this, the thing that immediately comes to mind is a delivery system of some design," Paul said. "With the new lines Creighdor has had built, he will have access to all of London."

"I agree," Narada concurred.

"But what would he deliver?" Emma asked.

"He could cause quite an explosion with the gas by itself," Jaijo said. "Instead of merely controlling the flow of gas throughout the city, it's possible he could turn those lines into a bomb."

"It's hard to own something after you've destroyed it," Matt said. "Creighdor's quest has always been one of acquisition and expansion. He has steadily built his holdings and clawed his way into the top circle of the financial arena."

"With building as his prestige," Paul said.

"He became a baron," Jessie said. "I don't see him just settin' that aside an' walkin' away from it after workin' for it so hard."

Matt's head hurt from thinking so much. They had been over and over all of this on the way back on *Swift Wind*. "He won't destroy anything. Unless he has to. He would use this gasworks of his to leverage something else. But the real question is, what is there for Creighdor to desire?"

"The throne," Gabriel said. "I think 'e might fancy gettin' 'isself a crown. 'E might like 'ow

'King Lucius I' sounds." He grimaced. "Doesn't quite roll off the tongue trippin'ly, eh?"

"No," Paul said, sighing. "But I do think you could be right. Not the throne so much, but controlling the queen and Parliament. I could see those as tangible goals for him. How would he accomplish that, though?"

"The lines were laid to deliver gas," Pasebakhaenniut said. "I would assume that whatever Creighdor plans, he would have to use that medium."

"Gas?" Matt asked.

"Yes."

"Gas is dangerous," Emma said. "As Jaijo pointed out, it's extremely explosive."

"The city is prone to fires," Paul added. "That is London's greatest weakness. We've still not properly forestalled that danger."

Pasebakhaenniut surveyed the blueprints. "Not the coal gas you're used to. Another kind of gas. A deadly agent that works on the nervous system. You can eradicate beings without harming the city's structures. Or the gold and assets."

"There's no such thing as a gas like that," Gabriel said. "You're talkin' about a fog or smoke that kills. Even coal gas is only dangerous when you're cooped up with it."

"Scientists are working with something very much like that now," Emma said. "It's called 'hydrocyanic acid gas.' Companies started selling it last year as a pesticide. It works on the nervous system."

"But we're not bugs," Gabriel protested.

"Unfortunately, the gas has proven harmful to humans as well, I'm afraid."

"Down in Texas," Jessie put in, "we've been usin' pyrethrum to control mosquitoes for years. There's manufacturin' companies in California. It's been used as a solution an' there's been talk of turnin' it into a gas."

"I don't know about those things," Pasebakhaenniut said. "But I do know that Creighdor and his species employ nerve agents in gaseous form while fighting land-based engagements." He looked back at the blueprint. "This is a huge delivery system."

"Would he kill the city, do you think?" Narada asked.

The mummy looked at them all. His eyes, and for the first time Matt realized the eyes had fully been reconstructed, were bright green in the center of startling whites. "If it suited Creighdor's purposes, yes. The city's streets would be filled with dead. But you have to consider Creighdor and his whole race. All they live for is war and overcoming all who stand in their way. With long lives comes the ability to think about plans that build over generations, not over night."

"But there are children," Emma whispered. "If he decides to destroy the city, the children will be victims too."

"Creighdor doesn't care," Matt said, knowing she was thinking of her own younger brothers and sisters. He felt the weight of impending doom. Creighdor's machinations had exceeded everything he had considered. His father had been right in fearing for the whole country.

"Even if we could convince the populace a danger existed," Paul said, "we'd never get the city emptied in time."

"No," Emma agreed. "And there would be several who would refuse to leave their homes."

"There's some who can't," Gabriel said. "The poor an' the homeless, they already got nowhere to go."

"Then there's no choice for it," Matt stated quietly, looking at his friends, knowing that all their lives were on the line. "We have to find Creighdor. Now."

"Matt," Paul said, "there are miles and miles of underground tunnels supporting the gasworks."

"Then the sooner we get started," Matt said, "the better." *Even if it is next to impossible.*

"Did you meet with success on your little treasure hunt, Matt?" Baroness Csilla Erzsebet Irmuska Kardos sat across the coach from him. They were outside one of the small cafés frequented by the shop girls who worked in Cheapside's textiles factories. Early morning light barely filtered in through the heavy curtains of the coach's windows.

Matt had been able to put off seeing her for two days while he searched the underground catacombs. He was bone-tired, yet struggled to remain awake while sitting with her. Everything in him cried to be up and about. However, he knew he needed to talk with her.

"We did." Matt looked into her amethyst eyes and felt drawn to them as he always did. *If things had been different between us, it would have been interesting to better explore the fascination with her.* And with everything going on in his fight with Creighdor, never a worse chance to have his interest deflected.

"What did you find?"

"A strange box," Matt said. She didn't know about his alliance with Pasebakhaenniut, and he wanted to keep it that way. She'd had a very adverse reaction to the mummy when they'd met, and pulling her further into his confidence was out of the question as long as Jessie and Emma were dead set against her.

Not that they didn't have their reasons, he told himself. He hated being torn between his friends and his own needs and wants. It wasn't a pleasant position to be in.

"Do you know the purpose of this box?" she asked.

"Not yet."

"Perhaps I could take a look."

Matt smiled at her. "I didn't know you were so mechanically inclined."

Csilla twirled a curl of her chestnut hair. "I have many talents you've yet to learn."

"Perhaps I will," he told her. "One day."

"I wish you would confide more in me."

"I don't want you pulled into this any further than you already are, Baroness."

"And I keep telling you that I'm already involved as deeply as I can be. Lucius Creighdor is my mortal enemy, as he is yours."

"If things were different . . . ," Matt said.

"But they aren't."

"No."

She sighed resolutely. "Tell me about the box. Creighdor evidenced much interest in it if he kept you alive to find out about it."

Matt had told her about his incarceration in the asylum. She'd been properly horrified and had told him she'd had her men out searching for him to no avail. He had left out all mention of the mummy, claiming to have managed his own escape.

"There's not much to tell," he said. "The box maintains its secrets despite our best efforts."

"I could help. After all, I saw some of the equipment Creighdor used while in Budapest after my friend had been killed."

"I have faith in Emma."

A pout formed on Csilla's face. "I could do so much more for you."

"Then wait," Matt encouraged. "Wait until the time is right."

She stared at him for a moment, then smiled. "Of course, I will. I feel very fortunate that we have formed this alliance."

"As do I, my lady," Matt said. Early morning traffic called him into action. He'd barely slept for a handful of hours and only then because he could no longer go on. He took his hat up from his chair. "Now I must be off."

She leaned forward, took him by the elbow, and kissed him. The intimate familiarity shocked Matt.

"Don't be so taken aback, Lord Brockton." She smiled. "Your customs here—are very rigid. In Budapest, showing affection is not tantamount to a crime."

"I meant no insult, Baroness," Matt said.

"None was taken, Lord Brockton. I kissed you for luck. Stay well until you meet me again."

"I will," he promised her, then he stepped out into the crowded streets of Cheapside. Her coach was in motion, taking her away, even as he turned around with his hat in hand.

Three of Gabriel's lads hooted and jeered at him, drawing the unwelcome attention of several shop girls who employed swift kicks to scatter the boys. Matt followed the boys, not looking forward to another day spent in the tunnels that honeycombed the city.

• • •

The next few days were a horrible nightmare of sleepless hours and anxiety. Gabriel recruited several of his lads to explore the gasworks tunnels, but even their numbers seemed pitiful in light of the immense underground search they had to perform. After dividing up the sections, Matt and the others led exploration parties. Even then they had to remain wary of potential guards and traps.

Lucius Creighdor and his schemes seemed invisible.

In the end, though, Creighdor's men found Matt.

They came for him just as he reached one of the dead ends marked on the copies of the blueprints Paul had gotten. Three of Gabriel's lads were with him, the oldest of them not quite ten. They were of little help in a fight.

The tunnel was one of the oldest, built with an arched roof that allowed the gas pipes to hang from their moorings and remain accessible to repairmen. The bricks that made up the walls and ceiling were irregular in size, cast by hand rather than on an assembly line. The surface was rough.

Josiah Scanlon, tall and lean and possessing a corpse's pallor, led the four men who seemingly came from the blank wall.

Matt and Gabriel's lads carried lanterns as they walked. Even so, their light barely touched Scanlon and the others as they erupted from the dead end.

The boys squalled and streaked for cover even as Matt shouted for them to run. He stood his ground, hoping to provide enough of a diversion to allow them their escape.

Recognizing one of his mother's killers, Matt dropped the lantern and tried to pull the Webleys from his coat pockets. He almost had them up when Scanlon smiled and fired something that blazed with green lightning.

Two prongs struck Matt's face. One of them hit his left cheek, and the other nearly embedded in his right eye. Wires led back to the tubular device in Scanlon's hand. Desperately, Matt aimed his pistols, knowing they wouldn't do anything to Scanlon. He squeezed the trigger anyway.

The bullets struck Scanlon and rocked him backward, sending sprays of green sparks flaring. Scanlon kept coming. He lifted the tubular device connected to the prongs in Matt's face.

Twin green fields lit up and shot along the lines to the prongs. When they touched Matt, it felt like his face exploded.

Blackness engulfed him.

Chapter 21

Groggy, Matt grew aware of the pain throbbing inside his skull. It felt like a wild animal fighting to be free. That made him think about the mind parasites, and he wondered if he'd been infected with one. Horror brought him up into a sitting position. Either the pain or the thought of mind parasites didn't agree with him. His stomach protested and spasmed, then he threw up.

"Well, well, Lord Brockton," Creighdor's mocking voice said. "I see you've returned to the land of the living." He paused. "However so briefly."

Squinting through the bright light focused on him, Matt dimly made out Creighdor's tall, thin figure. Grimly, Matt wiped his mouth with his coat sleeve. Seeing that he was still in his coat, his hands went down to his pockets.

"I'm afraid you no longer have your

weapons," Creighdor said. "You see, where you are, you're not going to need them."

Even the knife in Matt's boot had been taken. But Creighdor's men hadn't found everything. In spite of the impossible situation, Matt almost smiled. Thankfully, another spasm ripped through his stomach and doubled him over again.

"Not exactly a stellar moment?" Creighdor said.

"You'd be better served to kill me," Matt said in a hoarse voice. *Time,* he told himself. *You only need to buy a little time.*

That was the plan. If Creighdor nabbed any of them searching the underground, all they needed to do was live long enough to reach Creighdor's lair. When they had begun the search, they had known Matt would be the one Creighdor would most likely attempt to capture. They were gambling Creighdor would want to know what they had found in the North Sea. Pasebakhaenniut had said that Creighdor wouldn't let the opportunity pass by to learn what he could.

Matt gazed around the small room he found himself in. It wasn't a cell, exactly. More like a storeroom. But it was new, not something that had been around as long as the most of the tunnels he'd been in.

"I've killed the rest of your family, boy," Creighdor said. "I intend to make it a full set." He leaned in, lifting a lantern to show his vicious shark's smile devoid of humor. "I didn't get to see your father's last moments. I didn't get to make him beg for his life. Your mother begged, though. Of course, she begged for the life of her baby. Or did you not know about that?"

Anger flared through Matt, pushing away the sickness that twisted his stomach. He lunged at Creighdor, arms outstretched.

Creighdor moved incredibly quick, sidestepping and allowing Scanlon to move in and knock Matt to the ground with a baton.

The familiar blackness sucked at Matt's mind. He struggled to his hands and knees. Then Scanlon pulled him up by the coat collar.

"Did you know your mother was with child?" Creighdor taunted.

Scanlon held a knife to Matt's throat. The man's eyes were dark and flat with threat.

"She was," Creighdor said. "The child would have been a sister. Perhaps you would have liked having a sister. Or would you have preferred a brother?"

Glancing at Scanlon, Matt saw the man had shoved the Webley pistols into his belt. Another weapon, angular and long, with a gleaming surface, hung at his hip. *Just a little longer,* he told himself. *Surely only a little.*

"I knew your mother was with child." Creighdor motioned to Matt. "I . . . made adjustments to the child without your mother's knowledge."

"James Dorrance was your tool," Matt grated.

Creighdor grinned. "You have been busy, boy."

Matt said nothing.

Touching his hand to his chest, Creighdor said, "I used your unborn sister to remake my own body. It was important that her genes match mine closely enough. I had Dr. Dorrance conduct genetic matching tests, then some alteration that was necessary."

Matt distanced the pain and rage inside him. There would be time for both later. For the moment he clung to his father, remembering Roger Hunter had endured this battle for seven long, torturous years. *If you could do it for years, Father, I can do it just a few more moments.* He hoped that his friends would be quick. Or that Csilla would be quicker.

"It's funny, in a way," Creighdor said. "We're close enough to be brothers, you and I."

"Never," Matt whispered.

"Yet we have the same mother." Creighdor laughed again. "In a sense."

Scanlon forced Matt into motion, following Creighdor out of the small room into a larger one. Scanlon kept the knife tight against his throat.

The larger room was a maze of new pipes. They ran across the ceiling thirty feet above, like the ornate pattern of a spider's web. From there, Matt surmised, they branched out to the rest of

London. But inside the room all the pipes connected to a gleaming metal chamber in the center. Three other metal chambers, all of them huge, clustered around the biggest one.

Several of Creighdor's men and a dozen gargoyles stood in the room. Some of them stood along the catwalk that surrounded the room.

"You know I'm not human," Creighdor continued as they walked down the catwalk. "At least, not human as you are. I don't have the same weaknesses that your species has. Nor do I have to bow to the weight of time. My people learned the secret of immortality. Of course, we have to sacrifice others so that we may live. It's no small sacrifice. Such a pursuit for so many keeps us busy conquering other people, other worlds. Where I come from, I'm hated."

"You're hated here, too," Matt said.

"Perhaps," Creighdor said. "But those people also fear me. You and your lot, you've not learned to fear me enough. Not yet. But given time—and an empire—I will be." He gestured toward the chambers. "Do you know what this is?"

Matt didn't answer.

"This is a mixing chamber for a gas I concocted," Creighdor went on, beaming pleasantly. "A most unpleasant gas. Once released, it tends to destroy the self-will of anyone who inhales it. They become tabula rasa. Blank slates." He shrugged. "Of course, I can write on those slates, but the people become little more than automatons. Frankly, I don't care much for ruling automatons. They don't fear you enough."

Matt gazed at the cylinders. Pasebakhaenniut's drawing of what they were looking for was a close approximation of what Matt saw before him. Given the level of technology available, the mummy had been certain the delivery system would be more elaborate.

"Come this way, Lord Brockton. There's someone I'd like to introduce you to." Creighdor walked to the right.

Scanlon grabbed Matt by the hair and yanked him around, still holding the knife to Matt's throat. He was shocked when he saw whom Creighdor introduced to him as the other person standing there.

"Surely," Creighdor said with a smile, "you've met Queen Victoria."

The queen looked regal and imposing as she sat in a high-backed chair. She was in her late sixties, frail and nervous. Her gray hair was carefully coiffed.

Matt had first met the queen when he was a boy, while in his parents' company. That had been twelve years ago. She had been strong and forthright, and she'd loved to laugh. But that had been before Prince Albert, her husband and the love of her life, died ten years ago. During that time, the queen had lived in self-imposed exile, grieving over her loss with her nine children.

Only this year, during the Golden Jubilee of her reign, had the queen once more stepped into the public eye. Her popularity with the people had been at an all-time low. But this year she had managed to draw them back and win them over.

Now she was in the hands of a madman.

"Yes," Matt whispered, suddenly worried about everything that was about to happen. So much of it was about to be out of his control. He bowed slowly, avoiding slitting his throat on Scanlon's knife. "Your majesty, I apologize for the dire straits you now find yourself in."

"You?" the woman exclaimed. "You had something to do with the position we now find ourselves in?"

"No, your majesty," Matt said. He remembered the reverence his father had always had for the queen. "I have nothing to do with your presence here. If possible, I would see you clear and safe from this current situation."

"Unfortunately," Creighdor said blithely, "such an accomplishment is quite far removed from Lord Brockton's purview. I am your host."

The queen gave him a look of seething disgust. She had always been one to speak her mind. "You are a loathsome abomination. The first thing we shall do upon our return to the palace is strip from you the title we gave you."

Creighdor laughed. "You old biddy, you'll do nothing of the sort."

The queen's eyes widened in shock.

"In fact," Creighdor said, "you'll do exactly as I tell you to do or you'll die." He paused. "Mr. Scanlon, an exhibition, if you please."

Scanlon took his knife from Matt's throat and waved to one of the men nearby. The henchman left and returned with a glass-topped coffin. Inside the coffin, a bound man struggled. He wore the uniform of one of the palace retainers.

"Herbert," the queen gasped.

Creighdor took a hose from the main mixing chamber and affixed it to a valve on the coffin. He opened a valve, and a light green fog filled the container.

The man tried to hold his breath. He struggled, throwing his shoulder against the glass. The coffin remained intact.

In little more than a minute, the man took a breath. The green gas pulled in through his nostrils. Affected immediately, the man convulsed, jerking and shivering. Then he went limp.

Creighdor attached another hose and evacuated the gas. When he unsealed the coffin, the man continued to lie there.

"Climb out," Creighdor ordered.

Obediently, the man started struggling to climb from the coffin. Scanlon had to free his hands with the knife. The rope fell unnoticed to the floor. The man stood silently.

"Herbert," the queen said.

The man turned to look at her.

"Help us," Queen Victoria ordered.

Herbert stared at her.

"I'm afraid he can't," Creighdor said. "The effects of the gas have terminated his conscious mind. He'll never be able to think for himself again. He'll obey me because the machine inside the coffin attunes him to me. Specific commands will trigger a response, although a somewhat limited one, and any order requiring comprehension or creative thinking simply lies outside his domain."

A look of horror touched the old queen's eyes.

"So you see, your majesty," Creighdor gloated, "you can rule over a country of idiots, or you can start listening to me."

"To what end?" the queen asked softly.

"London *is* the most important city in the world," Creighdor said. "At this point. A man can build an industrial empire here that will impact this whole planet." He smiled confidently. "With your help, I intend to be that man." He paused. "More than that, I intend to repopulate this world, make it over in my own image, so to speak."

Horror grew inside Matt as he listened. Thoughts of Creighdor's twisted medical experiments collided within his skull.

"I've kept myself alive for thousands of years," Creighdor said. "Only lately have I recreated the process my people use to increase their numbers to fight their wars." He nicked his finger with a small knife and drew forth a drop of bilious green blood. "Inside this small drop are the genetic keys that I can use to remake several of your people.

"My people are at war far out there in the stars," Creighdor continued. "Our numbers have been diminished by the Protectors and their keepers, but those numbers don't have to stay diminished. The Protectors have hunted us down on worlds where we became vulnerable. But this place"—he shook his head and smiled—"they don't even know this place exists." He shrugged. "Maybe it will take a few generations, maybe it will take a hundred, but I will help accelerate technology. If your people don't develop space traveling vehicles on your own, then I will help develop it. I have time. That is the one thing my kind has always given itself, one thing that even the Protectors can't take away from us."

A stronghold, Matt realized as the truth of what Creighdor planned took root in his mind. *He plans to build a stronghold of our world and create troops to battle Pasebakhaenniut and his people.* "You're insane," Matt whispered.

"Actually," Creighdor replied, "I'm really quite clever. Re-inventing all these processes has been hard and time-consuming. Unfortunately, only a small percentage of the population can be cannibalized to remake in my image." He grinned. "You're one of the fortunate ones, Lord Brockton." He came over and touched Matt's face. "I'll take great joy in husking your body and taking what I need to make me over and over again."

Matt jerked his face away.

Turning his attention to the queen, Creighdor asked, "So what is it to be? Do you wish to be Queen Mother, however temporarily, to a new race of supermen?"

"What will happen if we don't aid you in this endeavor?" the queen asked.

"Then I will go into your children's bedrooms," Creighdor threatened quietly, "and I will personally kill each and every one with my own hands. Then I will flood all of London with this gas. In the morning, they won't know who you are. Either way, I'll get what I want. You have lost your prince, your majesty. Are you prepared to lose your children and your kingdom as well?"

"No." The old woman quavered, melting under Creighdor's fierce gaze. "We are not prepared to do that."

"Capital!" Creighdor exulted. "Then we understand each other perfectly." He shifted his attention to Matt. "Now for you, young Lord Brockton. I want to know what you found in the ocean, you simpleton. Did you reach that sunken ship?"

"Yes," Matt answered. If he was to die or have his mind horribly erased, he wanted to see the fear his knowledge caused Creighdor. "We did. The ship's cortex was there, Creighdor. We found it."

Creighdor's face turned into a mask of rage. "You know it is the ship's cortex?"

Matt made no reply.

"How did you come to know what it was?" Creighdor demanded.

Matt spoke calmly and coldly. "We weren't alone. Pasebakhaenniut went with us."

Creighdor's anger melted then, like snow under rain. Fear took its place.

"The mummy still hunts you," Matt stated. "I helped him find that device, and it will bring about your end."

Gesturing to the glass-topped coffin, Creighdor said, "Put this wretch in that box."

Knowing he had nothing to lose, that dying was preferable to living as Herbert was, Matt spun on Scanlon, ducking away from the knife at his throat. But before he could get clear, other men rushed in on him. He punched and kicked in an effort to get free, but there were too many of them.

Inexorably, Matt was stuffed into the coffin and the lid was sealed. He slammed his fists into the glass, hoping to break out. But the glass was too thick.

Creighdor leaned down over Matt and laughed at the coffin filled with the greenish fog. Desperately, Matt held his breath.

"Good-bye, Lord Brockton." Creighdor's voice was muted and drowned out by the hiss of gas that obscured his mocking features.

Chapter 22

Just as Matt was about to inhale his first breath of the mind-robbing gas, the glass top of the coffin shattered. He was in motion at once, leaping free of the falling shards as his lungs ached and burned. Only then did he hear the rifle shot that shattered the glass.

As he rose from the coffin, Matt glimpsed Jessie Quinn hunkered down on the catwalk, her Winchester already to shoulder as she fired again. The passageway she'd come through was behind her and to the left.

Where are the others? Matt wondered automatically. Jessie wasn't supposed to have come through the passageway. It was too dangerous. They had all agreed on that. *What has gone wrong?*

Her second bullet caught Josiah Scanlon in the right shoulder, staggering him, but Scanlon turned, drawing a strangely made pistol from his hip.

Matt threw himself at Scanlon just as a green

beam burned from the pistol. The beam turned the section of the catwalk where Jessie was into twisted, burning metal. The iron bars glowed red-hot.

Then Matt collided against Scanlon, knocking them both to the ground. Matt came up on top, one hand closed round Scanlon's gun wrist and the other balled up into a fist that he rammed into Scanlon's head. He knew he wouldn't have much of a chance before the other men overcame him. But as he punched and punched again, Jessie laid down a covering fire with the Winchester that was nothing short of impossible. Men twisted and spun away as the rounds hit them. Some were human. Others showed green smears of alien liquid.

Matt focused on Scanlon. This was one of the men who had killed his mother. He kept his rage pushed away, fighting as methodically as he had learned while in the East End at Gabriel's side all those years he had been without a father. *A calm head*, his father seemed to whisper in his head. *Despite the nature of the emergency, a calm head always prevails.* Matt hadn't heard those words in a long time, but he heard them now.

Scanlon looked up at Matt and grinned. "You're not good enough, boy." He surged up, throwing Matt off.

Even as he flew backward, Matt managed to grab one of his Webleys from Scanlon's belt. He fell backward as Scanlon stood and lifted his beam weapon. Reacting by instinct, Matt lifted the Webley, took aim, and fired three times in rapid succession. The large-caliber bullets tore through Scanlon's neck, separating his head from his shoulders.

Scanlon's body shrank inward, turning into a mass of whirling green flakes that disappeared. Behind him, Creighdor took shelter behind the queen and scuttled off into the darkness with her.

Matt heaved himself to his feet. Emotion ran raw in him as he realized one of his mother's murderers had paid the final price for his guilt and the other was getting away.

Another man crumpled, but this one bled red blood. As Matt grabbed his other Webley, he spotted Gabriel and Paul as they entered the big room on the catwalk. Both of them carried Enfield rifles and fired them at Creighdor's men.

Two of the gargoyles launched themselves into the air. Fortunately, their massive wings didn't give them much room to maneuver. Matt remained kneeling and took deliberate aim, firing his right-hand weapon dry.

His bullets destroyed the lead gargoyle's head and it fell and shattered against the ground. Paul's bullets hit the second one before it reached them.

The victory appeared to be short-lived, though. From somewhere in the darkness, Creighdor called his men to arms in a thundering voice: "Kill them! Kill them now!"

Matt thrust his empty Webley into his pocket and hefted the beam weapon Scanlon had employed. It was constructed simply enough, with a trigger. He fired his other Webley and the otherwordly firearm at the nearest men.

The bullet knocked one man backward while the beam burned a fist-size hole in the next man's chest before turning a section of the wall near Creighdor's head into molten slag.

"Be careful of the cylinders!" Creighdor commanded to his man. He took cover behind a thick stand of machinery. "Don't puncture the mixing cylinder! You'll release the gas into the room!"

Gunfire pinned Matt down behind the stairs leading up the catwalk to where Paul, Gabriel, and Jessie were. Matt fired the foreign pistol several times, destroying three more gargoyles as the creatures flew up toward his friends.

Creighdor's men didn't heed his warning. They rushed in among the cylinders and took up positions, firing again and again. Before they had a chance to concentrate their fire, a new front opened up at the other end of the room. In the uncertain light of the lanterns that lit the room, Matt barely made out the familiar figure leading them.

The baroness was dressed all in black. She moved among Creighdor's men like a wraith, fighting with pistol and sword as if she'd been born to them.

Jessie pounded down the stairs to join Matt as

Creighdor's men turned to deal with the newest threat. "The baroness?" she asked as she thumbed fresh cartridges into her weapon.

"Yes," Matt said.

"How did she find this place?"

"My idea." Matt plucked at the elbow of his coat and pulled free a small device the size of a needle. "The baroness had a tracking device similar to the one Pasebakhaenniut put on each one of us." She had put it on him the morning he'd last seen her. When he'd found it and realized what it was there for, he'd left it, counting on her to find him. He knew his friends, and especially Pasebakhaenniut, wouldn't have agreed to involving the baroness.

The second case retrieved from *Scarlet Moon* proved to be a treasure-trove of devices of otherworldly manufacture.

"You knew?" Jessie asked incredulously. "An' you allowed her to follow you?"

"Where else was I going to find an invasion force to occupy Creighdor so we wouldn't get killed out of hand?"

Jessie grinned at him. "You, Matt Hunter, are some piece of work."

Matt grinned back at her. "I do rise to the occasion."

Jessie took aim at one of Creighdor's men who was falling back from the baroness's forces. "We can't trust her."

"No," Matt agreed, and he felt a pang over that.

Csilla definitely had her own agenda. "Where are the others?" He fired the Webley at a group of men racing toward their position. Creighdor's men were like rats abandoning a ship.

Jessie levered the Winchester and fired again and again while answering. Her aim was lethal, dropping men in short order. But Matt knew it wouldn't be enough. Creighdor's men had superior numbers.

"It takes a while," Jessie replied, "to get those explosives ready. And to put them in the right place. That's why Paul, Gabriel, and I came down. So Pasebakhaenniut, Narada, Jaijo, an' Emma would know better where to put them. Pasebakhaenniut called it 'triangulation.' Course, I mentioned that we could die in the passageways before we got here. He said he could still use our positions, along with yours, an' figure out where to put them." She grinned grimly. "I didn't figure on dyin'."

Staying behind the stairs, Matt fired deliberately. Then he noticed tendrils of the greenish fog leaking from the mixing chamber in small clouds. The gas spread.

He looked at the three other chambers attached to the main one, then took aim with the beam. He held the trigger down and laid down a swath of fire that sliced the chamber from the main one. It fell with a clank, spewing blue fog into the air that quickly swirled near the ceiling.

Separating the chambers would prevent the gas from mixing.

The beam weapon suddenly felt hot in Matt's hand. He tossed it aside, thinking that something was going wrong. As it skidded across the floor, it exploded in a whirling green fireball.

Then, just as Creighdor's men had pinned them down so they couldn't return fire, another explosion shook the underground chamber. The ceiling blew downward, raining brick and mortar over the main cylinder. A twenty-foot hole opened up, showing the interior of the building aboveground.

"A tenement," Jessie yelled over the noise of the falling debris. "We had to clear it before we set the explosives. That's what took so long."

Everyone in the room hunkered down in silence for a moment, fearing that the entire chamber was about to collapse. Greenish fog poured from dozens of holes in the mixing chamber and moved sluggishly upward. Then Narada and Jaijo pushed a wagon over the edge of the hole and it tumbled inside.

The wagon plummeted to the floor. Heavy canvas kept its cargo mostly intact.

"Get down!" Paul yelled as he and Gabriel joined them behind the metal staircase.

Matt dropped and clamped his hands over his ears. He opened his mouth as Emma had suggested to equalize the pressure inside the room.

They had brought two wagonloads of dynamite. One was to break through the street foundations. The other was to destroy Creighdor's deadly apparatus.

For a moment, Matt wondered if the wire leads to the blasting caps on the dynamite had come loose. They had attached several in just such an event, knowing that it would only take one or two to set off the whole load.

But then the world seemed to come apart as the dynamite detonated. Flames whooshed out several feet in all directions. The destruction was limited to primarily the gas chambers and the immediate surroundings. Several of Creighdor's men were blown clear.

When he turned around, Matt saw the mixing chamber and the other two cylinders had been transformed into twisted hunks of metal. A steady stream of green fog spilled out, lifting into the tenement at street level. Once there, the chill winter wind tore the fog to shreds. Emma had guessed that the fog would dissipate in the prevailing breezes and become inert. Watching as the fog vanished, Matt felt certain she was right.

Glancing at Paul, Matt said, "Creighdor kidnapped the queen."

"The queen?" Paul looked astounded.

"Yes."

"Are you sure?"

"I was there with her." Matt ran toward the chair, knowing that Creighdor had to be somewhere near by.

The baroness's men battled what was left of

Creighdor's forces. They were almost at a stand-still until Pasebakhaenniut arrived with one of the beam weapons. The mummy marched among them like the specter of death, claiming lives with every shot. Bullets tore at him, but the silvery gleam rushed over the wounds and began knitting them at once. More of the gargoyles appeared and went straight for him.

Emma, Narada, and Jaijo peered anxiously over the edge of the broken ceiling. Then they fired at Creighdor's forces as well.

"Matt!" Gabriel cried.

Turning, Matt saw the young thief examining a portion of the wall.

"There's a 'idden door." Gabriel ran his hands over the wall. "See 'ere? Smoke's uneven."

Sure enough, the blast pattern caused by the explosion had left powder residue on the wall. Gabriel's clever fingers found what he sought. "A-ha!" he crowed in triumph. Then the wall section flipped inward, exposing a hidden tunnel. "Canny little fellow, isn't 'e?"

Matt didn't know if Gabriel was talking about Creighdor or himself. He took a fresh grip on the Webleys and charged through into the darkness, following the incline of the tunnel up to the street level to an alley.

The queen lay in the alley.

At first Matt feared she was dead. Then Queen Victoria flailed weakly. He rushed to her side and found that she was overcome.

"The knave left us, Lord Brockton," the queen gasped.

"Which way did he go, your majesty?" Matt helped her into a sitting position.

Queen Victoria pointed toward one end of the alley. "That way, Lord Brockton. Do be careful. He is a madman and a murderer."

Matt took off at once, calling over his shoulder, "Paul, Gabriel, see that the queen is tended to." He raced for the end of the alley with Jessie at his side.

Out on the street, a crowd had started to gather. Matt guessed that some of them were residents his friends had rousted from their homes. But others were neighbors who had gathered to gawk.

Creighdor shoved his way through them, screaming threats and waving his pistol. He fired at a coach driver, sending the man twisting from the seat. Without slowing, Creighdor vaulted up into the driver's seat and whipped the team into motion, scattering a dozen people standing nearby. Two male passengers leaped from the coach and went rolling.

Matt ran after Creighdor, shouting for everyone to get out of his way. He ran with everything he had, determined not to let his family's murderer escape. His breath burned his lungs, but he forced himself on, driving his arms and legs.

Jessie lost pace with him.

Matt didn't dare turn to look to see what had

happened to her. His concentration rested solely on the villain he pursued.

The coach turned the corner, the ironbound wheels skidding and sparking across the cobblestones. Pedestrians who had crossed the street to see what all the commotion was about ran away. Creighdor whipped the horses, pulling ahead for a moment.

Matt almost gave up hope. The London Bridge was just ahead. If Creighdor made it to the other side of the city, he could easily vanish. Matt wished Pasebakhaenniut were there. He felt certain even the coach would be no match for the mummy.

Then a milk wagon pulled out in front of Creighdor, causing the team to stumble as Creighdor roughly pulled them aside.

Matt gained the precious few feet he needed, throwing himself forward and catching the luggage rack in both hands. Only when he had his hold did he realize that he'd dropped his pistols. He pulled himself up the rack. One of the bags ripped open under his assault and nearly spilled him to the ground.

Clothing and other personal effects dropped into the street. But Matt's eyes lit on a gleaming length of steel—one of the passengers had packed a selection of rapiers.

Matt seized the weapon and pulled it free. The sword was nearly a yard of gleaming steel. A savage part of him took pride in the prospect of the damage he could inflict. He set himself to the climb again, swinging haphazardly from the back of the coach.

The familiar gridwork of the London Bridge was overhead when Matt pulled himself up onto the coach. They were on the bridge now, and the team was lunging toward the other side. Matt stood, crouched, and swayed atop the coach.

Evidently Matt's added weight alerted Creighdor, who turned and saw him. Consternation flashed in the black eyes. Holding on to the horses' reins with one hand, Creighdor lifted a pistol and fired.

Matt dodged to one side, but there was precious little room to maneuver on top of the bouncing coach. The bullet hit him in the side, burning briefly, then going numb. He staggered and almost fell, but he forced himself to stand.

Creighdor fired again, but the hammer fell on an empty cylinder as Matt threw himself forward. He caught Creighdor by surprise, but hoped he wasn't about to be shot dead.

Catching Matt's sword hand in his fist, Creighdor shoved him back with his superhuman strength, then tore the rapier from Matt's grip. Looping the reins over the brake, Creighdor came off the bench with the sword in his grasp. He swung the rapier at Matt's left hand.

Matt released the hold, desperately reaching for the luggage rack at the end of the coach with his right. He caught hold of the leather straps, aware of the broad Thames River on either side of the bridge.

"You're going to die, boy!" Creighdor roared. "Do you feel it?"

Matt scrambled to the rack. Then gunshots cracked, and Creighdor stumbled back, gazing down in disbelief at the green splashes on his coat.

Even riding bareback on a horse she'd apparently liberated from a coach, Jessie's sharpshooter skills were phenomenal. She closed the distance. Another rider was behind her, coming up fast.

Creighdor popped a small Derringer from his wrist and fired both barrels quickly. Blood spurted from Jessie's horse's head. The animal dropped almost immediately, turning in on itself. Jessie was flung free.

By that time, though, Matt ripped another rapier from the bag in the luggage rack. He heaved himself back on top of the coach.

Creighdor turned to him and snapped the trigger on the Derringer again. Nothing happened. Growling in disgust, Creighdor threw the small hideout pistol away and came at Matt with the rapier.

Matt fought with all the skill at his disposal, though Creighdor was an accomplished swordsman—but the man had never fought atop a coach hurtling along the London Bridge.

Matt moved his blade rapidly, guided by

instinct and experience. He parried and riposted, lunged and withdrew, always working toe-to-toe against Creighdor. The steel glided, razor-edge on razor-edge, barely missing flesh.

"Don't fret, boy," Creighdor taunted. "You'll join your parents soon enough."

Matt knew it was true. He was growing weaker while Creighdor showed no weakness. Pasebakhaenniut hadn't put in an appearance. Evidently the mummy was still busy fighting off the gargoyles in the basement.

Knowing he was at his end, Matt blocked his opponent's blade, going chest-to-chest with him. If he failed, though, Creighdor would disappear yet again.

"Now, boy," Creighdor taunted, his eyes black with anticipation.

"Now," Matt agreed.

Only instead of withdrawing, as Creighdor had expected, Matt lunged forward, planting both feet solidly, gripping Creighdor's coat in his free hand. His effort sent them clear of the hurtling coach, over the side of the bridge and toward the river.

Surprised, falling, Creighdor flailed with his free hand, worried about what lay below. He forgot about the fight for a split second.

In that second, knowing it was all he had, Matt struck. He freed his rapier, then swung the blade at his enemy.

The razor-edge sliced through Creighdor's

neck, severing his head from his shoulders. Incredibly, Creighdor's lips mouthed the word "Noooooo!" but no sound issued.

In the next instant, Matt fell through the green flakes that were all that remained of his arch-enemy. He hit the water hard, sinking at once. He was dimly aware of something else striking the water. He continued to sink, too weak to swim now.

He stayed beneath the water, going deeper. *I beat him, Father. We beat him. And we saved her majesty the queen in doing it.* He felt at peace, accepting.

Death didn't scare him. Somewhere on the other side of that great darkness, his parents waited. And his sister, whom he had never known. His work, the mission his father had given him, was at last done. His family had been avenged. Creighdor was no more. Now it didn't matter what happened to him.

Then arms slid under his and pulled him to the surface. Taking a deep breath, he looked around and found that Jessie and Csilla had him. They struck out for the closest shore, at the other end of London Bridge.

Together, they stumbled up through the mud into the docks. Glancing back in the direction of Creighdor's hidden gas factory, Matt saw flames reaching up into the night.

"Looks as though I happened along at the right time," Csilla said, smiling.

"Twice," Matt agreed. A pang of sadness touched him as he looked into those beautiful amethyst eyes.

"You knew I would be there tonight," Csilla said.

"Yes. I found the tracking device you put in my coat."

She smiled. "You're too clever by half, Lord Brockton."

"Too clever for my own good," Matt agreed. Slowly, he reached out and touched the greenish smear on her face that seeped from a cut. He drew his fingers back and showed her what he'd found, what he had known to be true. "You're one of them. Like Creighdor."

Jessie drew her Colts in a heartbeat. Matt held his hand up, signaling her not to fire.

Disappointment showed in the baroness's eyes. "Not like Creighdor. Not anymore. I've embraced this place and come to love many things about your world."

Matt shook his head. "You're still alive. In order to do that, you've had to kill others, sacrifice them to meet your needs. Truly, you're no better than Creighdor."

She smiled. "I let you live."

"It suited your needs. You needed me to run Creighdor down."

"You needed me," she said. "To help you in your attack tonight."

"Yes."

"Now what?" she asked.

"The choice is yours," Matt told her. "Pasebakhaenniut will take you into custody or kill you if he catches you here."

Out on the bridge, a coach sped toward them. Matt already made out the mummy in the driver's seat with Emma beside him.

"Then I can't be here, can I?" Csilla smiled sadly.

"Not if you want to be free," Matt replied.

"It would be nice," she said, "if things were different. You're kind and generous, Lord Brockton. And a capable and relentless warrior. You don't often find those qualities in the same man. You do fascinate me."

Matt didn't say anything. He didn't know what to say.

Without warning, Csilla stepped in close, grabbed the back of his head, and kissed him. Then she was gone, a shadow fleeing among the docks.

"Lettin' her go might not be the smartest thing you could have done," Jessie said quietly.

"I know," Matt replied. "But under the circumstances, it was all I could do." He sat then, feeling suddenly very tired. The wound in his side still bled, and pain was starting to return.

"Pasebakhaenniut's not gonna be happy," Jessie said.

"Then maybe we shouldn't tell him," Matt suggested.

Epilogue

Ornate cherubs carved into the gravestone stood out in bold relief on the stone vault. The inscription was brief and simple:

EVE ANGELINE HUNTER
1880
SLEEP, SWEET BABY
BELOVED DAUGHTER AND CHERISHED SISTER

It stood to the side of her mother's vault. It was, Matt hoped, where his mother would have wanted his sister to rest.

The quiet ceremony was conducted on the Hunter estate, in the family mausoleum. The parson and the few family friends departed under Finsterwald's guidance.

Matt stood with his friends at the graves of his family. The Chaudharys, Paul, Gabriel, Emma, and Jessie stood with him. Gabriel was dressed in a suit that Paul had lent him, and he looked very much out of place.

"You named her," Emma said softly. It was the first time she had seen the gravestone.

"Yes," Matt replied. "I felt she needed to be remembered." He took a deep breath, holding back the emotion that filled him. It was hard standing there facing all he had lost. "My mother loved the name Eve. She said if she ever had a daughter, she would name her Eve. I also named her for her mother, as my father would have insisted."

"It's a beautiful thing that you've done," Jessie said.

"She doesn't lie there, of course," Matt said. "No body was ever found."

"But you know she lived," Narada said. "This way, your sister, Eve, can be remembered."

That had been why he had had the symbolic burial performed: to give himself peace of mind. To provide Eve a final resting place where he could visit and think of her.

A month had passed since the explosion that had rocked all of London. Queen Victoria had quietly charged Scotland Yard with inventing the story of an accidental gas explosion that had killed Lucius Creighdor, Lord Sanger. No one was the wiser in the end, although rumors persisted of demons flying out of the hole in the ground.

In another ceremony, this one filled with

pomp and vigor, Queen Victoria had dismissed all charges against Matt and had knighted him in recognition of his steadfastness to the crown. Being in the news for good deeds, Matt came to find out, was less interesting to the general populace than scandal.

Matt said good-bye to his parents and to the little sister he would never in this life know, then walked from the graveyard with his friends.

"So where do you go now, Sir Matthew?" Paul asked, smiling a little.

"I don't know." Matt looked over the family estate. So much had been untended for so long. "I suppose I should oversee this place and get it back into good order. You tell me that my businesses are prosperous again."

"They could use some attention, though, my lord. It's not like you don't have anything to do."

"An' if you're ever up for a lark," Gabriel offered, "I know a couple thievin' weasels what's due a good comeuppance. Me an' you, we could teach 'em a thing or two, we could."

"What's that?" Jessie asked, pointing up.

Matt looked and saw the massive balloon floating through the sky.

"It's a hot-air balloon," Emma said. "Someone's aboard."

Minutes later, the balloon landed. Matt and Gabriel sprang to tie the basket to a couple of stout oak trees. The passenger turned out to be Pasebakhaenniut.

"Rudimentary flying craft," Pasebakhaenniut said, "but it got me here." He stepped from the basket and looked at Matt and his friends. "Have I arrived at a bad time?"

The Protector's "autonomous surgeons" still strove to return him to human countenance and had, for the most part, succeeded. He would never be handsome, never be more than a cadaverous caricature of a man. But at least now he no longer truly looked like the walking dead.

"No," Matt said.

"Good," Pasebakhaenniut said. "I find that after thousands of years in slumber, life is no longer simply a matter of going where you want." Even his diction had changed. "I have located another of the escaped prisoners."

For a moment, Matt's heart stopped. He still wasn't quite sure how he felt about Csilla. Nor had Pasebakhaenniut said anything on the matter of her escape.

"A man named Bucher," Pasebakhaenniut said. "It appears he's set himself up as a baron in Munich. I can't get to him by myself. I was wondering if you'd be interested in lending a hand. I can assure you he's every bit as bad as Creighdor. Murders have been taking place there for some time. Given the current state of German affairs, removing him with all due haste would be good. The trouble he's causing is only going to spread."

Matt glanced back at the graves of his family,

thinking about how much he had lost and how people hadn't believed his father or him. Finding people to believe in all the atrocities the Outsiders could cause was difficult if not impossible.

"I've also found leads on one in Shanghai and others in South Africa," Pasebakhaenniut said.

Matt looked at the Protector. "I will come," he said quietly. It was what his father would have done. For all intents and purposes, it was the Hunter legacy to track down the Outsiders and protect their world. Matt was determined to carry out that legacy.

The others quickly agreed.

"After all," Emma said, "we have formed a league. Bound by blood and belief." She put out her hand.

The others put their hands in as well.

Despite the pain over the loss of his family, Matt Hunter knew he was not alone. He would never be alone again. He placed his hand on top of the others'. "We will fight," he stated quietly, "so that others may live. I can't think of a more noble deed."

ABOUT THE AUTHOR

Mel Odom is the author of many novels for adults, teens, and middle-grade readers. He lives with his family in Oklahoma. Visit him at www.melodom.net.

When Gus González is adopted by a famous TV star,
he expects to be living the good life,
not running for his own.

A novel from Simon Pulse
Published by Simon & Schuster

Printed in the United States
By Bookmasters